FORWARD

My Story

FORW

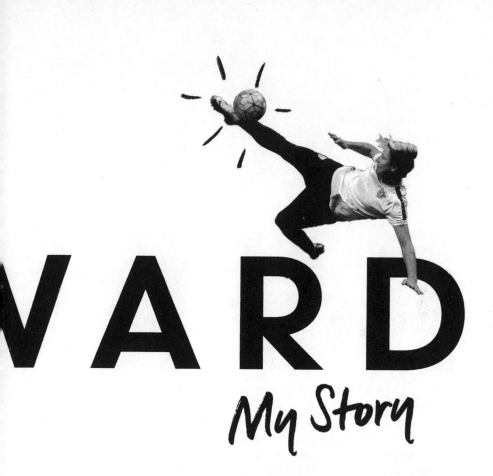

VARD
My Story

ABBY WAMBACH

HARPER
An Imprint of HarperCollinsPublishers

"Untitled" by R. M. Drake reprinted by permission

Forward: My Story (Young Readers' Edition)

ISBN 978-0-06-245792-9

16 17 18 19 20   PC/RRDH   10 9 8 7 6 5 4 3 2 1
❖
First Edition

Dear Abby,

Before there was soccer, championships, applause, jeers, heartbreak, shame: there you were, four years old.

Today I want to hold you and promise you this:

Don't try to earn your worthiness. It's your birthright.

Fear not failure. There is no such thing.

You will know real love. The journey will be long, but you'll find your way home.

You are so brave, little one. I'm proud of you.

Love, Abby

FORWARD
My Story

CONTENTS

FRAUD

I HAVE SCORED MORE PROFESSIONAL soccer goals than anyone else in the history of the game—184, to be exact—but I never once witnessed the ball meet the net. Although my eyes were open and aimed in the right direction, the second I hit my target the picture went black—not a slow fade, but a swift chop that separated the scene from my ability to see it.

For thirty years, scoring goals was the one skill I could count on for security and acceptance and love. Rarely did my brain pause long enough to consider what might come next, and how my life would look without soccer to fill it up.

Now it's November 2015, two weeks after I announced my retirement. I have let soccer go, but it hasn't let *me* go. And today, my life still isn't what I'd imagined it would be, but I'm starting to appreciate the view.

In these pages I will share plenty of tales from the field—ones I have never told before—but this is not, at its core, a book about soccer. Admit it: No matter who you are or what you've done in your life, you recognize a feeling I'll describe in these pages: that private, constant worry that makes you wonder if you're lost for good. You have, at some point, experienced setbacks and been forced to find a way to re-create yourself. You've found yourself in the midst of transition, working up the nerve to take your next step. You have been treated unfairly and unequally. You have been labeled, placed into ill-fitting boxes, and told by others what you are and how to be. You have even labeled yourself, lessening your potential with your own words.

Here are just a few of my labels: tomboy, lesbian, coward, failure, control freak, rebel, fraud. And a few more, on the flip side: inspiration, captain, champion, advocate. At a young age I learned that you own labels by defying them, and you defy them by owning them. I know that the final word on me will be one that I choose.

Seventy-seven of my unseen goals came courtesy of my head, and I am often asked to explain my technique: how my body knew where to be and how hard to hit, how I sensed and made the connection. For me, soccer was, and is, a complicated, chaotic dance, one that demands the repetition and mastery of its steps. In every game, in every play, my chance of scoring was directly related to my memory of previous goals. From past experience, I could predict the ball's path and position my head to meet it, finding the sweet spot just before everything went dark.

Soccer has taught me many lessons, but the greatest one is this: Sometimes the only way to move forward is by first looking back.

TOMBOY

MY SIX SIBLINGS AND I were raised on competition. Tales of diligence and strength and success were passed down like cherished heirlooms. We heard about my great-grandfather, who bought a wooden stand, piled it high with colorful triangles of fruit, and waved down each wagon passing through upstate New York. My grandfather improved on the idea, trading in the wooden stand for a building and twenty-two acres of land, naming the business Wambach Farms. When he died he left everything to his only child, my father, who, after his high school graduation, began working at the store seven days a week.

My father would stop work long enough for

dinner and come home at 6 p.m. sharp before heading straight back to the store. His nightly presence at the table was one of the official family rules, a list controlled and made longer by my mother over the years. Another rule was the mandatory head count, instituted after my brother Pat was accidentally left home alone (like Macaulay Culkin in the movie) during an outing to a local restaurant.

Even manners were a contest; it was widely acknowledged that the Wambach kids were the nicest and best behaved in all of Pittsford. Our town was a conservative, suburban community just outside Rochester, heavily Catholic and wealthy, and we were to obey its unspoken code. We had to be polite to neighbors, strangers, and elders: We sent handwritten thank you notes; we were told to hold open doors; we never mouthed off or said bad words. We attended Mass at St. Louis Church every Sunday, dressed in our finest, and sat in the front pew. "That priest up there?" my mom would whisper. "He's watching your every move. God is watching, too, so no monkey business." We behaved when my parents took their vacation in Florida, leaving us with our grandparents, occasionally for months at a time. We listened. We obeyed.

We understood and acknowledged how blessed we were because we were exposed to those less fortunate; every year, my parents enrolled in the Fresh Air program, inviting city kids to stay with us for the summer. I looked forward to those visits, eager for a glimpse of anything and anyone outside my daily life. On some level, I sensed that I was different, too—a difference that stretched beyond my usual abilities on the soccer field. I knew it would take time to understand how and why.

My mother's most cherished rule was: There will be order and calm at the dinner table. Designated family time was sacred. We were to share something about our day, one child at a time. My mother enforced this rule—and every rule—with what we all called "The Look": eyebrows pressed into a V; lips flattened into a line. The Look made her invincible, supreme, and being on the receiving end of it was punishment enough.

My mother named me Mary Abigail after the Virgin Mary, and she dressed me in ruffles and bows starting the day I was born. My father had been a gifted athlete himself, wrestling and running track and playing football. Before they began working full-time at the family store, I used to beg my four brothers to take me to the neighborhood cul-de-sac, cover me in goalie pads, and kick slap shots at me until sundown. My sister Laura was creative, free-spirited, and musically gifted. My oldest sibling, my sister Beth, was athletic, brilliant, and on her way to becoming an Ivy League–educated doctor. She was my second mother, always willing to tend to me when the real one ran out of time. After she left for college I became so sad and withdrawn that my parents took me to a psychiatrist.

Even then, I was beginning to realize that soccer was my secret weapon, my own unique way to get adoration and respect.

My father prodded me. "How many goals did you score today, Abby?"

I beamed at him. "A hat trick," I said. Three goals.

His response was swift: "Why not four?"

I had no answer.

I scored more hat tricks. I scored more times than I could count. I scored twenty-seven goals in three games and, at age nine, was sent to join the boys' league. They teased me, calling me "tomboy" and telling me to go back to the girls. I welcomed their treatment and longed to prove that I belonged. I played football with my brothers and their friends, tackling one neighborhood kid so hard I left him moaning on the ground. I added basketball to my schedule and discovered that it helped my soccer game. During my weekly phone call with Beth, she would always ask if I had won my latest game.

"Sure did," I'd reply. "Thirty-two to nothing."

"That's great! How many points did you score?"

"Thirty-two."

I started experimenting with headers, taking note of how the ball launched from my scalp. My father ordered me to move from central midfielder to forward, since forwards have more opportunities to score. In eighth grade, I was recruited to start on the varsity team for Our Lady of Mercy High School, the private, all-girls institution that my sisters attended. I started participating in the Olympic Development Program, or ODP, which gave me exposure to college and national team coaches. I gave my first interview to a local television station.

"Where do you get your athletic talent?" the reporter asked.

"My mom played zero sports," I said. "But my dad was one of the fastest runners in New York State."

With each passing day soccer became a bigger part of my life. I loved it for what it gave me: praise, affection, and, above all, attention. When I was on the field I didn't have to beg to be noticed, either silently or aloud; it was a natural by-product of my talent. I hated it for the same reason, terrified that soccer was the only worthwhile thing about me, that stripping it from my identity might make me disappear. My future teammate and friend, Mia Hamm, would one day offer this advice for players just starting out: "Somewhere behind the athlete you've become and the hours of practice and the coaches who have pushed you is a little girl who fell in love with the game and never looked back. . . . Play for her."

I was not, and never would be, that little girl. Already I knew I was incapable of falling in love with the game itself—only with the validation that came from mastering it, from bending it to my will.

I hated soccer even more when my mother declared that I had to skip my vacation at Stella Maris, the Catholic summer camp I'd attended for as long as I could remember. My heart sank. I was fourteen and not yet ready to let go of being a kid. It was the one place where I could do crafts and play tetherball and not think about soccer. Instead, she said, I had to go to soccer camp and work on improving my technique.

This wasn't the first time we disagreed. A part of me was still angry about her long trips to Florida. *You came back and now you want to be my mom?* I'd think. *You haven't been here!* To her alarm, I started refusing to wear dresses, even to church. On Sunday mornings, I would pull on sweatpants, making her panic. I knew I'd get The Look, and she delivered it on cue. But I dug in, refusing to budge. I might have inherited a sports gene from my father, but my stubbornness came from her. The strategy worked brilliantly as a bargaining tool, as a way to find middle ground with her, and when I slid into the front pew at church I was wearing pants and a shirt. She blamed my behavior on a desire to be like my brothers, and I wanted to tell her, *No, this is all me.* I wanted her to love me anyway.

But with soccer, there was no compromising.

"Mom," I'd plead, "I need to learn life. And I need to learn life through my mistakes, too. My life can't be all of your choices. If I make a mistake, I want it to be *my* mistake."

My mother remained unmoved.

I huffed off to sulk in my room but was stopped by my brother Andy on the stairs.

"I'm going to quit soccer," I announced.

He dropped his hand on my arm, held me still, and spoke to me in a tone I'd never heard before.

"You have such a gift," he said. "You have to accept that. You can't quit. You would be doing all of us a disservice. We all wish we had half of your talent."

I felt like I was being asked to choose between soccer and myself, and I wasn't sure how—or even if—one could exist without the other. I was determined to have both.

In the end, I agreed to spend my summer at soccer camp, all the while plotting other ways to rebel.

REBEL

I BEGAN TO REVOLT LITTLE by little, tiptoeing around the edges of soccer without attacking it directly. I was playing five days a week for Mercy High School, two games and three practices, and I challenged my body to see how much abuse it could take. Every morning on the drive to school, I steered my hand-me-down Chevy into McDonald's for a breakfast sandwich and a Coke, the first of at least a dozen sodas I'd drink that day. On a dare I devoured an entire stick of butter. I'd scarf large orders of chicken wings, then hold the box up to drink every drop of grease that had pooled at the bottom. One time before practice, I ate fifteen fried pizza rolls and then ran a timed mile, throwing up as soon as I hit the finish line. I once rode a Jet Ski straight into a lightning storm.

I became the only child my mother didn't trust, a fact she shared openly and often. None of my brothers or sisters ever had a curfew, but she made mine 11 p.m., a full hour before my friends had to be home. If I pulled into the driveway at 10:45, I'd sit there and wait so I wasn't a second early. Once, while my mother was in Florida, I got my tongue pierced. As I left for school, she planted herself between me and the door.

"You have a tongue ring," she said. "I want it out of your mouth and sitting on this table by five p.m. or I'm going to sue the pants off that place you went to."

I didn't want to be on the news for my tongue ring, so I did as she asked, but our fights became more and more explosive from then on.

"I wish you were dead!" I'd scream at her, and she'd spin on her heel and order me to her "office"—a small bathroom on our main floor. When she'd close the door I'd expect The Look, but instead she'd be expressionless, all her features fixed into place. She'd speak with terrifying calmness and clarity: "One day when I *am* dead, you are going to regret saying that."

My grades were terrible. Instead of listening to my teachers I practiced my autograph, filling my notebooks with hundreds of ornate *Abby Wambachs*, picturing the lines of future fans. I realized my eyes focused differently, one nearsighted and the other farsighted. That helped my soccer game, allowing me to gauge the ball at every distance, but always made reading difficult. My eyes fought against each other, exhausting my brain.

I knew I only had to do well enough to get into college, and that college would be paid for by a full sports scholarship. I didn't behave badly when it came to soccer. On that subject alone I respected my mother's wishes, listening to my coach, Ms. Boughton, and obeying her every order. In my sophomore year she made me captain and motivated me with insults.

"Get on your horse!" she'd yell. "Stop being so lazy. You're not playing to your capability. You're not displaying the level of sophistication a leader should have. I don't care if you want to quit." I tested her, telling her often that I never wanted to play soccer again. Panicked, she'd call my mother, who'd laugh and say, "Just give her time." To Coach Boughton's relief, my mother was right: In two weeks I'd be back on the field, chasing the ball with my head.

No one had ever spoken to me like that in my life, and I gratefully took in every word. I was tired of hearing about my talent and was desperate to know my flaws; I wanted to corner and confront them and use them to help me improve. I wanted to be better, if only because being better got me more attention. I was the last kid left in high school, and my mother had time to come to my games, chatting with the other parents in between blows of the whistle.

In my mind, her conversations were all about Beth: the smart one, the responsible one, the first great athlete of the family, who led Mercy's basketball team to a state championship; Beth's name, in fact, was on a banner in the gym. In my mind, my mother's biggest question was whether I could win the championship, too, and I took it as a challenge. *If I win, maybe she'll love me the most. If I win, maybe I'll finally love myself.*

I had a boyfriend, my first, and he told me he loved me all the time. His name was Teddy Barton and he played soccer for McQuaid, the companion boys' school to Mercy. Teddy had dark eyes and long, shaggy brown hair that he tied up in a ponytail. My parents approved of him: He was a smart, athletic kid from a good family, a future Navy pilot, already looking ahead. They even invited us to double-date with them at their country club, where they'd take pride in the fact that the servers and members all knew my name.

We were the unofficial "jock couple" of Rochester. His friends became my friends, even when I outplayed them on the field, but I pretended not to hear their jokes: *Teddy, your girlfriend is bigger than you are. Teddy, your girlfriend is gay.*

I *was* tall—I grew ten inches within a year and stood five foot eleven—but I was not gay. At least I didn't *think* I was, since I wasn't sure what "gay" felt like, or how that identity would fit if I tried it on. On the walls of my room hung posters of the usual nineties heartthrobs, Brad Pitt and Tom Cruise, and I wouldn't have minded substituting Teddy for any of them. When he took me to a Dave Matthews concert, the singer kissed me on the cheek and I refused to let Teddy touch that spot for the rest of the night. I was still a tomboy, but no more so than any other female athlete at my school; we all wore backward baseball caps over our ponytails. I thought I loved Teddy, but then again, I wasn't sure what "love" felt like, either.

On the night of his senior prom, my mom was thrilled at the sight of me in a dress and heels, which made me much taller than Teddy. We danced for hours, and he begged me to stay out late, but I had a game the next day and needed to be home by curfew. Within the week my best friend, Audrey, called me, saying she had a hypothetical question.

"What if you knew your best friend's boyfriend cheated on her?" she asked. "Would you tell her?"

"When did Teddy cheat on me?" I replied, bluffing.

A part of me didn't think he was capable of it.

"Oh! I didn't think you'd figure that out."

"He did?" I asked. "When? Who?"

It was after I left prom, she said. A girl from a different school.

I ignored him when he begged for forgiveness, and I was surprised by my reaction: My pride was wounded more than my heart.

One day after soccer practice, my parents and I stopped at the Macaroni Grill. I still remember my outfit: white turtleneck, blue corduroy pants, Doc Martens, and a bright yellow North Face jacket I'd saved up to buy. Our server approached, wearing a crisp white shirt and skinny tie. She had long brown hair and green eyes and seemed to be smiling only at me.

I couldn't look directly at her, but I couldn't look away. I *liked* her. I liked her in a way I had never liked Teddy.

I don't remember ordering, or what my parents talked about; there was a booming silence in my ears as my heart pounded against my chest. I could feel the energy in my arms and legs; my feet tapped and my fingers shook. When she walked away to get our drinks, I picked up a crayon from the table's basket and doodled a soccer ball, willing myself to be calm.

I felt like a switch had flipped inside me, blinking neon and sharing my secrets to the whole world.

When she came back she was still smiling at me, and she pointed at the soccer ball I'd scrawled on my place mat.

"Oh, you play soccer?" she asked.

"Yes, I play soccer."

"That's super cool. I played lacrosse and soccer."

I told her I attended Mercy High School, and she asked if I knew the famous soccer player who went there, the girl who was always on the local news.

"I know her," I said. "That's me."

I learned her name was Stephanie, and when she cleared our plates her hand skimmed my pinky finger, a touch all the more powerful because it happened so quickly.

I silently repeated the three syllables of her name all the way home.

I paced in my room, back and forth between my window and my door. *What was that?* I didn't know what to do with the feeling I'd had around her. For a moment I wondered if it was just my latest attempt to rebel, and in a way I knew would hurt my mother the most. If I liked girls, I was a bad Catholic, doomed for all eternity.

The feeling was worth the risk. I sat down at my desk and typed a letter, picking my words with care:

Dear Stephanie,

I was one of your clients today, and we got to talking. I can't really tell you who I am, and I don't know what this feeling is about, but I want to get to know you. I've never done this before. If you know who this is, look me up in the phone book and please call me.

Without knocking, my brother Andy barged into my room.

"Get out!" I yelled. "I'm doing something personal." Hunching over the letter, I turned my face just enough to scowl at him.

I could tell he was curious, but he backed away.

I mailed it to "Stephanie, c/o the Macaroni Grill."

I waited, and held my breath with each ring of the phone. On the third day Stephanie called.

"Hey!" she said. "This is Stephanie from the Macaroni Grill."

"Cool," I said, trying to sound calm. "How are you?"

"Well, I got this letter. And I wondered if the letter was from you."

"A letter?" I acted surprised. "What letter?"

"Oh, you didn't send a letter to the Macaroni Grill? My bad, so sorry."

I laughed and said I was just joking with her, and it

was me. I knew right then that whatever this feeling was, she had it, too.

We began to see each other secretly. I didn't tell anyone, but a group of local girls found out; one morning I found a rainbow sticker slapped on the back of my Chevy Blazer, and I scraped every last bit of it off. I went to great lengths to hide my relationship from my teammates and friends. Once, on the way back from a soccer game in Syracuse, I stopped at Stephanie's house and lost all track of time, missing both family dinner and my curfew. My mom called Audrey's house to ask if she knew where I was. For once, she didn't. Neither did my friend Breaca, who was offended that I kept my secret from her. When I got home I made up an excuse, and if my mother didn't believe it she kept it to herself.

Throughout senior year I heard daily from college coaches who wanted me to play for them. Each bragged about their program, their campus, their social scene; some jokingly promised me half of their salaries. My mother gleefully stuffed a binder with offer letters and brochures. I visited four schools, one right after the other—the University of North Carolina, George Mason, the University of Virginia, and UCLA—and I was convinced I should choose the one farthest away from home. "I'm done," I told my mother. "I'm going to California. UCLA it is."

"No," she said, offering a slightly different version of The Look. "I'm trying to honor the fact that you want to make this decision, but you have to make five visits. The reason you don't want to go on one more visit is because you're lazy."

"Fine," I finally agreed. "It's between Clemson or Florida, whoever calls first."

Without saying a word to me, my mother intervened. She decided that Clemson was "too Southern," and that, if I chose Florida, she and my father would be able to attend games when they were vacationing at their condo. She called Florida's coach, Becky Burleigh, asked her to hurry up and call me, and within a week I was off to visit Florida.

The university's soccer program was brand-new, a by-product of Title IX, the law that made it illegal for any federally funded school to discriminate on the basis of gender, including in the creation and development of sports programs. Later, I'd realize how fortunate I was to have benefited from the law, which enabled American women's soccer to dominate on the international stage; FIFA estimates that 12 percent of youth soccer players are girls, and US players make up more than half that number. During the nearly four decades from 1941 to 1979, women in Brazil were completely barred from playing soccer.

Even today, there's a stigma against female players, who are sometimes called "sapatão," a rude term for a lesbian.

But then, as an eighteen-year-old, I wasn't focused on the politics of soccer. I just liked the idea of building something from the ground up, of being the underdog with something to prove. It was settled: I'd be playing for the Florida Gators. My mother won the game without me even knowing we were playing one.

I was away on an Olympic Development Program trip when I made the decision, and my mother helped me orchestrate my announcement. She lined up sweatshirts from all five prospective schools along the kitchen counter and invited reporters to the house. At the appointed time, I called home and told my mother what she already knew. As she raised the Florida sweatshirt—number four in the lineup—over her head, everyone cheered and clapped. "I'm going to a movie now," I told her, knowing she was still basking in the spotlight.

In the last few months of my high school career I had just two things on my mind: the state championship and Stephanie. I knew our relationship would probably end once I headed to college, so I tried to see her as much as possible, sometimes letting it get in the way of soccer. During an away game for the U.S. Women's National Under-18 Team, I played poorly on purpose, missing headers and tripping over my feet and letting opponents slip past. When the coach questioned me, I had a lie already prepared: My beloved uncle was dying, and I really needed to go home. I had one ready for my parents, too: My ankle hurt, and I didn't want to begin my college career injured, so I had to come home and rest. As soon as I was back I went to find Stephanie. Our relationship was still a secret, but I knew soon enough I'd have to say it out loud.

She was there, watching, on the day Mercy High School played Massapequa for the state championship. More than playing for the Under-18 team, more than earning a full ride to college, more, even, than identifying what made me different, I saw a state title as the high point of my high school life. Winning would put my name up on a banner in the school auditorium, above my sister Beth's. Winning would correct my faults and fill in my gaps. It would make my mother see past all the parts of me she wished she could change, including the parts she didn't yet know.

We played on Astroturf after a snowstorm, in conditions that are unthinkable to me today, with a layer of slush still coating the ground. For the first sixty minutes the game progressed perfectly, as though I'd choreographed every move. I was playing better than I ever had, the ball kissing my forehead before it found the net, and we were up 3–0 with twenty minutes left. Couch Boughton pulled me aside and told me I'd be playing defense, and in my mind I thought that was crazy—playing not to lose instead of to win—but I did what my mother would want me to do, and I obeyed.

The minutes ticked by: nineteen, eighteen, seventeen. Massapequa scored three goals in quick succession, and for the first time in my life the game slipped away from me, operating on some level I couldn't reach. I saw their winning shot with cruel focus, soaring past me, past all of us, the scoreboard lighting up to confirm our defeat. My defeat.

I sensed myself growing smaller, my body curling inward, my elbows to thighs, my head to my hands, my ponytail grazing the ground. I felt the sting of snow through my stockings, numbing the points of my knees. I was wailing, making a noise I'd never heard, and it occurred to me that I'd never before cried in public; I was horrified at the thought that my emotions might be recorded and judged. I didn't know how long I was there before my teammates surrounded me, pulling me up an inch at a time. My legs felt separate, moving without orders from my brain, and they took me to the fence, where I saw my mother waiting, her body stretching out to

meet me. She pulled me in close, her hands touch-
ing behind my back, and she put her mouth to my
ear: *I love you, Abby*, she said. *I love you.*

I relaxed against her, finally believing the words
and feeling like I'd earned them.

TEAMMATE

ON THE NIGHT BEFORE I left for college, I sat with friends on my front steps until sunrise, finding shapes in the stars. I was eager to leave Pittsford, with its strict rules and expectations, with its unspoken hopes about who I was supposed to be. For all of my eighteen years I'd lived someone else's version of me, and I needed to create a new model of myself—one I recognized when I looked in the mirror.

"Tomorrow a whole new life starts for me," I whispered to myself. "I don't know when I'll come home again."

I was ready to see what was next for me.

My mother had packed up nearly everything I owned,

leaving only my trophies behind. She'd arranged each box in my new Jeep Wrangler with such tight order that not an inch was wasted. My father had struck a deal: If I got a full scholarship to college, he'd buy me the car of my choice. He argued for a BMW but I insisted on the Jeep, fearing judgments about arriving on campus in such a fancy car. He also offered to pay $50 for every college goal I scored, a big raise from my high school rate of $25. They followed me on the nineteen-hour drive down to Gainesville, making sure we weren't separated by more than one car. I was exhausted from my late night, and a few hours into the drive I started nodding off, swerving in and out of my lane. Loud honking woke me up, and through my rearview mirror I saw my mother waving her arms, motioning me to the side of the road. For the rest of the way, we took turns, one of my parents driving my Jeep while I slept in the passenger seat. My mother lowered the volume on the radio and shifted into fifth gear, working the stick with surprising ease. *Wow, when did Mom learn how to drive a stick shift?* I thought. I liked the idea that she had secrets of her own.

A few days later, at 5 a.m., I showed up at my first preseason practice totally unprepared. Over the summer Coach Burleigh had sent a packet detailing how we should condition ourselves, but I refused to put down the Coke and junk food, let alone go for a run. My teammates and I gathered at one end of the field and waited for the shriek of the whistle. If I didn't pass this fitness test, I wouldn't be allowed to play. But I was used to abusing my body without problems; it had never failed to do what I told it to do.

I was off: eight hundred yards in three minutes, around the track. I ran swiftly, surprisingly fast for a big girl, finding my rhythm. I had two minutes to rest, and I was barely out of breath. Next up: a back-and-forth suicide run—six, eighteen, and sixty yards—in thirty-four seconds. Halfway through and I could hear my mother's voice: *I told you to go for a run, Abby. I warned you this would happen.* The sun grew hotter each second, burning my scalp. Sweat dripped into my eyes. *I can't do this*, I thought, and then I was off again, running four hundred yards in 1:25, both painfully present in my body and feeling as though I were floating above it, a witness to my suffering. I gulped only three hoarse breaths during the forty-five-second rest, and I ordered my legs to run again. Another 6-18-60 suicide run, and my body began to revolt. I felt like I was going to throw up.

And then a terrible realization hit me: The workout was only half over.

I felt like I was physically incapable of running another step or taking another breath or bending to touch the ground with my fingers, but then my body did something it had never done—it took control and spoke to my brain: *I am not going to stop, even if you think I'm finished. You have so much anger inside of you, layers and layers of rage, each a different flavor. Feeling like a failure, feeling like a freak, feeling abandoned and unloved and unlovable, feeling like an "athlete" is your only authentic identity, a total far greater than the sum of all of your parts. Take that anger and use it now to make me move.*

My mind submitted to my body, and my body responded. I began to gain speed, overriding every scream and aching bone. Another four hundred in 1:25, another 6-18-60 suicide run, another eight hundred in 3:15. Through those last eight hundred yards I felt like I was going to pass out, but my mind fed its anger to my body, and my body absorbed it all, using every last bit of energy until they both, at once, ordered me to stop. It was finished. I did it.

I thought I might die, yet I had never felt so alive. I hid under my towel, fearful that if I looked up to watch the goalkeepers I might never be able to step on a field again—and I had to, in just a few hours, for more drills and a scrimmage. One of my new teammates, Heather Mitts, sat next to me. I lifted the edge of my towel to look up at her. She was a junior, two years older than me, with shiny blond hair and legs up to her armpits, and I suspected—correctly—that one day we'd be together on the U.S. National Team.

"I don't know if I can do this," I confessed.

She smiled, a quick flash of white teeth, and said, "Yeah, you can."

It was a dare as much as an order, and I believed I could do it—as long as my body and mind were speaking to each other.

Our team had twelve seniors, all of whom had been there from the beginning, when the program first launched four years back. They became my new family, substitutes for the older siblings I'd left back north, and I was equally desperate to please them. My pedigree—142 high school goals, one of the country's top-ten recruits, named the high school player of the year by numerous organizations—didn't matter on my new field. Unlike at Mercy, this team didn't depend only on me. Raw talent was no longer enough, and I needed to prove I belonged on this field.

Every horrible three-a-day, every scrimmage, every game was a chance to get their attention. I scored on a header in my very first game, a 3–0 victory. I credited my goals to teammates, knowing that without their skillful serves, I wouldn't score at all. At a game in Connecticut, a male fan began harassing a teammate who also happened to be gay. "Hey, twenty-eight!"

he yelled to me, referencing my number. "Is number eight your girlfriend?" I deliberately kicked the ball into the stands, a line drive that nearly collided with his head. He left her alone after that. I cheered everyone on as they ran their suicide runs, sometimes literally pushing them across the finish line. I stayed just fit enough to cross the line myself. *Look at me*, I thought. *See me. Notice me. Love me—if not for who I am, then for what I can do.*

What I wanted to do, what we *all* wanted to do, was make it to the NCAA tournament, where we'd likely meet the University of North Carolina Tar Heels, who'd won the championship game fourteen out of the last sixteen years. Every time we played the Tar Heels they dominated the field, beating us four times over the three previous years, scoring eighteen goals to our one. I had my own issue against North Carolina—its legendary coach, Anson Dorrance, was the only person who refused to offer me a full scholarship (he offered a partial, which, in my mind, was the equivalent of the cost of a couple of textbooks). The Tar Heels were a dynasty, a superpower that churned out stars for the national team like clockwork, and I was determined to play a role in knocking them down.

Early in our season it became clear that we had something; we *were* something, and we felt untouchable. We defeated teams we'd never beaten before—Southern Methodist University and Texas A&M and Vanderbilt—and as our first game against UNC approached, we saw no reason for the streak to end. In October, in front of five thousand fans— including my parents, who attended every game—it did end, but barely. One of our seniors tied the game 1–1 in the eighty-sixth minute and forced an extra period, during which the Tar Heels scored and won. But this loss felt different, like it was halfway to a win. It was our only loss of the season, and we prepared to meet the Tar Heels again.

Two months later, we did, in Greensboro, North Carolina, just fifty miles away from UNC's home field. It was our first time in the NCAA tournament, and just one game stood between us and the national title. We were ready, and within the first six minutes our captain shot a free kick, soaring the ball over the head of the Tar Heel goalkeeper and lighting up our side of the board. The next eighty-four minutes were some of the ugliest soccer I'd ever played, a ferocious stretch of hustle and vigilance and hurling myself at the ball, all 170 pounds of me tumbling forward and coming to rest on my face. Every minute stretched on forever, and toward the end, at the final TV timeout, Coach Burleigh summoned us together for a huddle. We placed our sweaty arms around each other's necks and fidgeted, stabbing at the turf with our cleats.

I looked at my teammates, one by one, as if I was back home in Pittsford at the dinner table, waiting for my chance to talk. This was the seniors' time, their last shot, and I was respectful of the team's hierarchy, being ready when they needed me and stepping back when they didn't. No one was louder or more insistent than the youngest of seven, and I decided that they needed me now, that some words were best said in my voice.

Rearing my head back, I roared: "We are *not* losing to UNC!"

When I lowered my face I saw everyone was looking at me. Coach Burleigh mentally threw out whatever speech she'd prepared and said, "Okay then. Let's go."

We ran out, whooping and slapping palms, and when the final buzzer sounded, my proclamation had come true: The score stayed steady, and we had won. In that moment, buried beneath a pile of screaming teammates, it was so easy to trust that my voice would never fail me.

LESBIAN

ONE NIGHT, I DECIDED TO tell my teammates that I was gay. They suspected something, I was sure of it; I'd heard them whisper, but not in a mean way. They were just curious. I was scared, but then I thought: *"Gay" is only one part of who you are, and you should be as vocal about that as you are about everything else.*

When I told them, they couldn't have been more relaxed. "I knew it!" they said, laughing, and then moved on to the next topic of conversation.

I still had my long blond ponytail, and guys hit on me regularly. Early sophomore year, at an athletes' party, one approached me. He was big, six-two and about two hundred pounds, and he told me his name was Are—spelled like the verb, but pronounced like the letters: R.E. For the next three hours, we talked and eventually concluded, with mutual delight, that we were the loudest, most obnoxious people in the room.

"I need to tell you something," I finally said. "This isn't going anywhere. I like girls."

"That's cool," he replied, and from then on we were inseparable.

I decided Are was me, exactly, in a slightly bigger body. He was my wingman as I negotiated my first "out" adult relationships. At a party early my sophomore year, I spotted a girl with long dark hair standing quietly in the corner. Her name was Nikki and she was a nationally ranked tennis player, and knew all too well the pressure of being forced to perform, the feeling of hating the very thing that brought you love. We connected over our mutual determination to have a life outside our sports, to be more than who we were on the court and the field. She was three years older than me, inching closer to deciding what she wanted to do with her life, and before long I was hoping, slightly terrified, that those plans would always include me.

Our relationship reminded me that I needed to

have a life outside soccer, and Are was a willing partner. When I wasn't with Nikki or on the field, he and I were sitting in my dorm room playing video games. He was as competitive as I was and always up for a contest. It was fun, never a battle.

My astrological sign is Gemini, and I have true twin personalities, always at odds with each other. On my right shoulder sat responsible, dedicated Intense Abby, serious about sharpening her technique and maintaining her fitness, always aware of her growing role as a leader on the team. On the left, whispering loud enough to fill both ears, was bad, rebellious Chill Abby, who argued that if I let soccer take over every aspect of my being, I would not be able to play at all.

Despite Chill Abby's triumphs, my game remained intact and the honors accumulated: two-time SEC Player of the Year, two-time SEC Tournament Most Valuable Player, first-team All-American three years in a row. I was on my way to setting a school record for goals, assists, game-winning goals, and hat tricks, and the national team coaches were taking notice.

During spring of my junior year I was selected to attend camp in California for the U.S. Under-21 team. There we scrimmaged against teams from America's first women's professional league, the Women's United Soccer Association, or WUSA. At the end of camp I was brought in to talk with Jerry Smith, the U-21 coach and the husband of Brandi Chastain, one of the stars of the 1999 World Cup–winning women's team.

I ran into Jerry's office, eager for his assessment.

"How do you think you did?" he asked.

"Well," I said, "I scored the most goals."

He nodded. "That's the hardest thing to do. How did the rest of your game go?"

There was something strange in his voice, as if it was a trick question, and I hesitated before I responded. "What do you think?"

"Terribly," he said. "You do the hardest thing to do in our sport better than anyone else here, but the rest of your game has a long, long way to go. You're unfit, you're a danger to the defense, and you're only good at attacking when you're in a scoring position. There's so much more to the game. You're here because you do the hardest thing the best, but if you want to stay with us you'll have to try a lot harder or I won't bring you back to camp. In fact, I'm not inviting you to the next camp. You have talent and I would love to invest in you, but you have to have more skin in the game."

I was quiet, considering his words. I longed for criticism, and yet I was reluctant to commit to what he asked of me.

"Is this meeting over?" I asked, finally.

"That's it," he said, and motioned toward the door.

One month later, back in Gainesville, I sent Jerry an email. "I thought about what you said," I wrote, "and it had an impact on me. If you bring me back, I'll show you."

He responded immediately: He had been hoping to hear exactly that.

My relationship with Nikki was as exhausting as back-to-back suicide runs. She'd graduated and moved to New York City, and we took turns dating long-distance and then calling it off. I was still insanely in love with her and desperate to make it work, but she was hesitant. I was the first girl she'd dated, and she wasn't sure if she wanted to be with a girl or a guy. I sent her love letters and gifts and offered to watch her dog, but I decided I'd never pressure her to come out to her family; I hadn't even come out yet to mine.

Intense Abby stepped in and argued that hard work and focus would be a perfect distraction from my romantic troubles. At the insistence of Coach Burleigh, who feared my poor fitness might ruin my shot with the national team, I made an appointment with Randy Brauer, a muscular therapist who trained the Gators' football players. We met by the track, and Randy told me to run, observing me from the sidelines. After one lap he held up a hand, halting me.

"Oh, no," he said. "Has anyone ever taught you how to run? You're leaving craters in the track." Not only were my feet improperly positioned, but my body was tightly coiled: fists clenched, brows furrowed, mouth pursed, shoulders raised to my ears. I needed to relax and stop fighting myself. Intense Abby was nothing if not coachable, and within two weeks my steps were barely noticeable, quicker and lighter than they'd ever been.

I tested them one day during a training session. One of Randy's athletes, a starring center for the football team, made a judgmental comment as I sprinted past. I don't recall what he said but I'll never forget his tone. Even though I'm totally comfortable in my skin now, I'm still judged in similar ways—questioning looks when I walk into bathrooms or through airport security, looks that require me to make my voice higher to say "Hi," and, if that fails, to declare, bluntly, "I am a *girl*." It happens so often that it's a joke to me and my teammates, yet a part of me—to this day—finds it hurtful, and wants people to pay better attention, to take the time to look. To *see* me.

But back in college, such comments, intentional or not, were not funny at all. Standing on that track, I remembered how far I had come. Right then, I was not in the mood to be judged.

The football player was a big boy, three hundred pounds, and could easily bench-press twice his weight. I ran down the field toward him with all I had, as if each step might be my last. He was on bended knee, studying his foot, and didn't even hear me coming until I was on top of him, knocking him over and crawling onto his chest. I was kicking and growling as we flipped and rolled across the grass. When he finally escaped, I rose up and thought: *Victory.*

I decided to take a step closer to becoming myself, so I told Are to cut my hair. He stood behind me, an electric razor in his hand. "Do it," I ordered, and he turned it on. My hair dropped in long blond ribbons, forming a shag carpet on his floor. Are's mother, Dena, stood to the side with tweezers. "You gotta teach me to pluck my eyebrows," I told her, and she did, starting on the left. "Ow! Ow! Ow!" As she pinched and pulled, I forced myself to ask her a question: "What would you do if your kid was gay?"

She stopped plucking and looked at my reflection in the mirror. "I would just hope they could find love and happiness," she said.

Smiling, I motioned for her to finish.

* * *

The next day, Are and Dena sat next to my parents at my game. My mother gasped when she saw me. "Oh my gosh," she said, elbowing my father. "Peter! I cannot even believe that's Abby's head. Oh my gosh. This is a tragedy!"

"A tragedy is the Twin Towers coming down," Are pointed out, "not Abby's haircut."

The shock of my hairstyle was nothing compared to the news that I wouldn't be graduating. With just a few months left of school, I was drafted by the Washington Freedom for the WUSA's second season. My parents helped me pack up my life in Florida and move to an apartment on the outskirts of Washington, DC.

I decided to take my mom to lunch at Chevys, a Mexican place near Pentagon City. I was sweating, the heat of my hands defrosting my chilled glass. She sipped her iced tea and looked at the menu. My heart thumped in time with the mariachi music. I could tackle a massive football player without hesitation, but I was deathly afraid of this woman. When I found my voice, it squeaked into the air higher than usual, and I felt like I was back in Pittsford, fighting against wearing dresses and surviving The Look.

"Mom," I said, and paused. "I've got to tell you something. I've been meaning to do this for a long time. I'm nervous, and I'm really sorry if this upsets you, but I'm a lesbian."

Her reaction was fast and unexpected. "No you're not," she said.

My body straightened in the booth. "Yeah, I am."

"Abby, no you're not."

"Yeah, I am."

She shook her head. "Abby, you just don't know what it's like to be in a relationship with a man."

"Mom," I said softly. "I dated Teddy, remember, and I'm much happier dating girls. I'm dating someone now, a woman. I've dated a few girls."

Her expression was serious and sad, as though she was caught between recognition and acceptance. She opened and closed her mouth, debating her next words, and then said nothing.

We ordered and ate, and for once in my life I didn't know how to fill the silence.

ROOKIE

EVERY DAY I WOKE UP and said to myself: *No one controls me anymore.* I made my own money, and it felt like a big amount for a twenty-two-year-old. I bought a chili-pepper-red motorcycle that I zipped around the streets of Georgetown. I made a few unfortunate fashion choices, growing my hair into a mullet and wearing a leopard-print cowboy hat. I was still on-and-off with Nikki, and she was still not out to her family; I understood but was getting impatient. I wanted a commitment, a plan for us. I wanted a future.

I craved some comfort and familiarity, so I invited my old high school friend Audrey to live with me. Chill Abby and Intense Abby were in balance, neither one overpowering the other. Chill Abby still ate and drank whatever she wanted, but Intense Abby was determined to excel at her new job with the Washington Freedom, to keep getting called to the national roster. No one controlled me anymore, but I still thought: *If I play well, my mother might forgive me for being who I am. If I play well, I might forgive her for wishing I were someone else.*

Despite feeling that, I became more open, and I came out to my Washington Freedom teammates without any hesitation. In fact, I made a joke about it, and everyone laughed, which was a big relief.

The star of the Washington Freedom was Mia Hamm, member of the legendary '99 World Cup–winning team and the most famous female soccer player in the country. Back in Pittsford, in my childhood bedroom, a signed poster of her held a place of honor over my bed. Mia's popularity was the main reason the WUSA existed at all. She was eight years older than I was, six inches shorter, forty pounds lighter, much, much quieter, and infinitely more terrifying than she appeared. The previous year, during my official start for the national team, I was called off the bench as a late substitute in a friendly match against Germany. For the entire eighteen minutes I played, Mia yelled at me—Where was I going? Why wasn't I moving? What was I doing?—and she approached me afterward, explaining that she knew I was tough enough to take it.

Before our season began, Mia had surgery on her left knee and was projected to miss the first ten games. Still, she was at every practice and match, screaming from the sidelines, and whenever I left the field she suggested ways I could improve. I was leaning too far back, she said. I was going over the bar. I needed to remember to check my shoulder. I should use my big body as often as I could. I still wanted criticism over praise, so I absorbed everything she said. When the season ended, I was named the WUSA's Rookie of the Year.

Secretly, I decided that the honor signaled that I could stop pushing myself and do bad things like eat too much and not work out. Chill Abby took a step forward, becoming my dominant personality. I got lazy and my body forgot how to move the right way. April Heinrichs, the coach of the women's national team, began excluding me from important games. One night she pulled me aside and told me I was unfit, I was slow, I was uncompetitive. If I didn't shape up, and quickly, I wouldn't be playing with the women's national team. I would miss the 2003 World Cup, my first.

I listened; I focused; I pushed Chill Abby away. I finished the Washington Freedom's season with thirty-three goals, the most in the league, and scored the winning shot at the championship game—the "golden goal," it was called, since it happened in overtime. Our celebration was short-lived; three weeks later, on September 15, the WUSA folded. The 99ers were beloved, but their fame was not enough to support an eight-team league—especially when the target audience, teenage girls, had their own games to attend. I was out of a job, and worried that we'd never be able to reignite that national passion for women's soccer, that our sport was destined to fail, that no one would ever care about us or take us seriously.

The World Cup was going to be played in the United States. Rides on the team bus were usually a big, crazy party, with my voice the loudest of them all; I channeled my nervous energy into singing (badly), dancing (even worse), and talking nonstop. Julie Foudy, another 99er and the captain of the national team, once gave me a T-shirt with the words: HELP! I'M TALKING AND I CAN'T SHUT UP. But this time the atmosphere on the bus was subdued, everyone discussing their private pressures and concerns.

Mia and Julie were hoping that a World Cup victory might revive the WUSA; if they played as well as they had in 1999, the sponsors might invest again. A few days earlier, I had been profiled in the *New*

York Times, with the headline calling me a "Mass of Woman," and the article positioning me as a potential breakout star for the team. Intense Abby was hyperaware of the expectations all around—and within—her. I was the one piece that was different from the '99 team, the new ingredient that was untested and unknown.

We started with wins: against Sweden, Nigeria, North Korea, and Norway. Despite the victories, the crowds were small and quiet. People were preoccupied with football season; more than that, the ghost of the failed WUSA seemed to haunt each stadium. On Sunday, October 5, we faced Germany at PGE Park in Portland, Oregon, just a few miles from where I would one day live with my wife.

From the beginning the game felt off, a dance where everyone was a half step behind. The day before, we had practiced set pieces, predicting how and where and when Germany would strike, but our opponents were not behaving as expected; they were delaying and cutting angles. I had a "mark," the player I was supposed to cover (and, in Coach Heinrich's words, "run over like a Mack truck"). Her name was Kerstin Garefrekes and she was five ten, just one inch shorter than I was, but lighter and leaner; my body could overpower hers in any showdown. I had studied the way she played and asked my teammates about her history, and I believed I could anticipate her every dodge and step. But somehow, in the first fifteen minutes, she moved in a way I didn't predict, positioning herself near the post. On a corner kick, she found the ball before I did and banged her head against it, bouncing it off the crossbar and into the net. They scored twice more, and we didn't score at all.

No matter that my mark didn't make the game-winning goal; I allowed her to set the tone. That thought attacked me with every bit of strength I had, and I couldn't stop thinking: *This loss is your fault.* It was the high school state championship all over again, and I wanted to disappear, to rewind my life back to a time before I ever pulled on cleats or headed a ball. Later that night, I spent hours in the shower, crying and beating my fists against the tile, but right then, my grief was private. I forced myself to stay on the field, watching my teammates cry while the Germans celebrated.

I felt an arm drop across my shoulders and heard Coach Heinrichs say, "Come on, let's go inside."

"No," I told her, my eyes still fixed on the German team. "I want to remember this."

MANIC

FOR THREE WEEKS AFTER THE World Cup I thought of nothing but that first goal, the goal that helped the Germans win, the goal I allowed. My mind replayed the moment on a continuous loop, an awful slideshow I was powerless to stop. Even the elements that were out of my control haunted me: I should have known how my mark would move. I should have beaten her to the ball. I should have hurled my body at her shot and deflected it from the net. I couldn't stop thinking: *My fault, my fault, my fault.*

I was relieved when Coach Heinrichs announced the Olympic roster and I was on the list. In February 2004, we started camp in Hermosa Beach, California, where I shared an apartment with two teammates. I began preparing for the challenge ahead. I got lots of sleep. I ate no sugar. In addition to soccer drills and scrimmages, I worked out twice daily at a training facility in the Home Depot Center. I watched my body wake up and change, the ridges of muscles rising up. With every weight-training session and lap around the track I reminded myself what was at stake: After these games, the 99ers were retiring. I ruined their final World Cup, and now I had a chance—no, a responsibility—to make it up to them, and to redeem myself in the process. By early August, when we'd leave for training camp in Crete, I'd be a different person.

My determination stayed even as my love life became unexpectedly complicated. Since the beginning of training, I'd noticed a woman who was working as a nanny for our assistant coach. Her name was Haley, and she was my usual type: confident, athletic, feminine. I had no idea if she was into girls until one day, when I stepped off the bus, she laid a hand on my shoulder. I stopped, my foot raised midair. *What the heck was that?* I thought, and tried to shake it off. I was still dating Nikki, and she was scheduled to fly in from New York for a visit. The last thing I needed was a breakup right when I was trying to stay focused.

The following week, during Nikki's visit, we were

out to dinner when my phone rang: it was Haley.

"Let's go take a walk," she said.

"Wait, *what*?"

I could hear her take a short breath.

"How about a walk?" she tried again, this time as a question.

There was nothing I wanted more, and realized I had two options: break up with Nikki as soon as possible, cutting our visit short; or string her along for the week only to surprise her when she got home. I went with number one, and Nikki flew out the following morning. But of course I still felt like a jerk when I picked up the phone and called Haley.

We met for dinner at a sushi place on the ocean. Afterward we strolled to the pier. It was closed, so we took turns jumping the fence, and we had miles of beach to ourselves, the ocean lapping at our calves.

She kissed me, and I fell in love instantly.

We saw each other as often as possible during training. Every time I traveled with the team I headed to her apartment as soon as I came home. I bought her gifts. We laughed and talked for hours. I wanted to know everything: where she'd been, where she was going, what she'd been through. She took every other thought out of my mind until it was time to leave for Greece. Only then did I remember the Germans celebrating the World Cup, and I brought that anger with me.

We were up 1–0 against Brazil in the final, but the game was not going well. The Brazilians were fast and animated, like we were at a dance party rather than the Olympics. Like it was fun and not war. We were slow and disorganized, failing to find each other, and the only reason we survived was because Brazil kicked the ball, twice, off the goalposts. With seventeen minutes left, our luck ran out: A Brazilian player named Pretinha, my former teammate on the Washington Freedom, shot a line drive into the net, tying the game.

The pressure fueled me, catering to my need for extremes; I did not know how to exist in the middle. I unleashed my old failures and let them run free inside me, filling me up with a wild rage. In the 112th minute, I saw my chance in the form of a corner kick, and I leaped, unfurling my long body, swinging my head—making contact, and then a sweet, momentary blackout before I realized what I'd done.

In the locker room, Julie Foudy turned to me. "Thank you," she said, "for not making the next forty years of my life miserable." Mia was next, and she spoke of leaving the program in the hands of the next generation. For the first time I realized that my life was about to change, for good. It was the beginning of my turn.

In the fall, after a nine-game victory tour with the national team, I planned something I'd never done before: a solo trip, two weeks of hiking and camping in the Arizona desert. For the first time in a long time I was at peace, both with my accomplishments and with who I was, and I wanted to hold on to that feeling, tuck it away for safekeeping. Even as happy as I was right then, I knew the day would come when I wouldn't be, and I'd need to remember it.

Then I picked up a car. I had a plan but I expected that I'd improvise, Intense Abby and Chill Abby in perfect balance. I started heading west, intending to stop first in Flagstaff. An hour into the drive, I felt an odd flicker of unease, a sudden and persistent sense that something was wrong. Panicked, I stopped at a gas station, loaded up on coffee and energy drinks, and drove thirty-two hours straight, taking a slight detour to Haley's house in Phoenix, where she was going to school. I couldn't help but break our newly enacted pact: We'd decided to take some time apart, and meet the following year in the Grand Canyon if we missed each other.

By the time I arrived it was sunrise, and I pressed her buzzer, holding my finger down until she appeared at the door. I was wild-eyed and exhausted and crazy, but I didn't care; I needed to see her expression in order to know the truth. I asked her to tell it to me, straight and honest, like we'd always been.

Taking my hand, she led me to the driveway, where we sat on the trunk of her car. She tilted her face toward mine and confessed that she was dating someone else.

"Who?" I asked, my voice sounding small and far away.

"You don't know him," she said.

Him.

I was too wired to cry, and instead I got in my car and drove the final two hours to Flagstaff. Lying sleepless under the stars, I tried to convince myself it was okay to be on my own.

A few days later, I stopped at a diner and realized it was Thanksgiving, the first I'd ever spent alone. I imagined my parents and siblings and their combined three dozen children sitting around the table, loud enough to be heard down the street. I slid into a booth, scanned the menu, and couldn't help but eavesdrop on the family sitting behind me—mother, father, and young girl, their plates piled high with turkey and stuffing. I turned my head just enough to estimate the kid's age, guessing she was about seven or eight.

"You really need to find a good man," the mother said, and I sat straighter in my booth. "You need to find a good man to have a good life, just like I found your father."

The words stirred a fury inside me. I thought about where I was: twenty-four years old, just a few steps away from being a powerful, empowered woman, someone who never considered relying on a man or anyone else for my well-being and success, someone with an Olympic gold medal.

I twisted in my seat, poking my head into their space. I opened my mouth and was prepared to start talking: *Lady, just shut up. SHUT UP. Don't lessen your daughter! What you're doing right now is giving her an out to rely on someone else, and in this world, if you rely on other people, they take advantage of you. If you rely on other people, you don't get to where you want to go. You get to a version of yourself, a small portion of yourself, and never learn how to access the whole thing.*

But I didn't say anything, and to this day I still think about that little girl.

DEPRESSIVE

IN MY CAREER AS A player, soccer had cycles that corresponded to cycles within myself. Several years of quiet work led to a few short weeks on the international stage, where, win or lose, we descended back down the mountain and prepared to climb all over again. After the high of the Olympics, followed by the news of Haley's betrayal, I craved that period of hibernation, the chance to feed myself in ways that had nothing to do with the sport. It was an escalation of the pattern I began in high school, when I first realized that soccer was bearable only if I took time to rebel against it.

When I got back to my old apartment in Washington, DC, I called Are.

"Where should I move?" I asked him. "Los Angeles or San Francisco?"

"LA," he said without hesitation.

After scouring the internet for a condo, I bought one, sight unseen, with my Olympic money, and told Are he was coming to live with me.

We moved in June 2005 and settled into an unconventional routine, grilling out every night and joining a touch football league, playing on the beach. I reconnected with Haley, talking regularly on the phone and traveling to Phoenix for occasional visits.

I met a new friend, Kara, who worked as the team's sports therapist. We were both Geminis, born four days apart, and she understood my dual—and occasionally dueling—personalities better than anyone. Right away I could tell she spoke her mind, even if the thought was one I'd rather not hear.

The dynamics on the team were changing as swiftly and dramatically as I was. We had a new coach, Greg Ryan, and only three of the 99ers remained: Kristine Lilly, Kate Markgraf, and goalkeeper Briana Scurry. Our new roster included a dozen players who were twenty-three or younger, and a dozen who had played in five or fewer games. At twenty-five, with sixty caps under my belt, I was a veteran, and I began to act like it, ordering people to hustle at practice and evaluating their play, being every bit as blunt as I was when I critiqued myself. The 2007 World Cup was still more than a year away, but I was already fearful of repeating the failures of the last one.

We started another residency training camp at the Home Depot Center, three weeks on and one week off. After practice one afternoon, a teammate casually mentioned Haley's engagement. I froze, my locker door half open. *Engagement.* I couldn't imagine why she would do such a thing without telling me, or even how she could do such a thing in the first place. Clearly she was willing to risk losing me for good. My mind went back to old, bad feelings: I was unloved. I was unlovable. I was abandoned and forgotten. Even if I forced myself to be seen, I would never truly be found.

As soon as I got home, I sat on the edge of my bed and summoned the will to call her, afraid of what I might hear. After three rings she picked up.

"Hal," I said, my voice cracking.

"Hey!" she said cheerfully, and I suspected she knew what was coming.

"I heard something really weird, and I don't know how to say this—it's so bizarre." I laughed meekly, as if the very thought of it was too crazy to consider. "Are you . . . *engaged*?"

She was quiet a moment, and admitted, "Oh, yeah, I am."

I needed to know every last detail. Her fiancé wasn't the man she had told me about before I drove off into the desert. This was a different man, a man she'd never once mentioned in all our long conversations. *This* man surprised her with a trip to Mount McKinley, hiking with her to the summit, where she turned to find him on bended knee. She kept talking, and every word was an internal earthquake, each more powerful than the last, carving a fault line from my throat to my heart and splitting me in half. "I still love you," I heard her say, "and that won't change."

"What?" I screamed. "How can you be getting married to this man when you have feelings for another person?"

"I'm different than you. I'm not going to lie to you and tell you I don't love you."

"Wouldn't you think I needed to hear that *before* you decide to marry him?" I was sobbing, and embarrassed that I'd allowed my emotions to escape.

She was quiet, out of things to say.

"I don't know how to process this," I whispered, and hung up.

CAPTAIN

THE CYCLE OF SOCCER SPUN forward, taking me along with it, and as the World Cup approached I emerged from hibernation, sharpening my focus. But for the first time in my career my body was not cooperating, opening itself up to injuries it had always managed to avoid. In early November 2006, during a tournament in South Korea, I leaped onto the ball and rolled my ankle so badly I thought it was broken. Just a sprain, the trainers determined, and after they gave me a cortisone shot and wrapped it in a thick wad of tape, I was good to go again. A few weeks later I scored both goals in a 2–0 game against Mexico, qualifying us for the World Cup.

I thought the worst was over, but it wasn't. Before

we left for Shanghai, during a warm-up game against Finland, my big toe collided with another player's leg. I could feel the toe swelling inside my cleat, throbbing against the leather, but I kept playing until the twenty-seventh minute, when it could no longer withstand an ounce of pressure. During the first game of the World Cup, with toe numbed and ankle wrapped, my head rammed against the head of a North Korean player, as solidly as a bowling ball striking a pin. The back of my head split open. Blood seeped from my scalp and trickled to my neck, and in this condition I walked 150 yards to the locker room at the end of the stadium for stitches. During the ten minutes I was out, our 1–0 lead became a 2–1 deficit, and we finished at a 2–2 tie.

Before the semifinals, where we'd be facing dramatic, show-off Brazil, Coach Ryan made a controversial decision, benching our goalkeeper, Hope Solo, in favor of Briana Scurry, a 99er who was set to retire soon. From start to finish the game was a disaster. Our set pieces faltered and failed. Our defense was tentative and full of holes. We lost a key player, midfielder Shannon Boxx, late in the first half after she received a red card. In the end we lost 4–0, and left in shock as the Brazilians tackled each other on the field.

On the bus ride back to the hotel, everything hurt:

my ankle, my toe, my head, my heart, my pride. This was not only my chance at redemption after the last disappointing World Cup, it was also my first major test as a leader of this team. Once again I'd let everyone down, myself included, and I felt dressed head to toe in failure, wearing my shame like a second skin.

I was back in my room, lying on my bed, when one of my teammates burst in. "Did you see the thing Hope said?" she asked. I hadn't but it was all over the news. In an interview after the match, Hope claimed, "There's no doubt in my mind I would have made those saves."

There's an unspoken code in our sport: You don't talk badly about your teammates; you don't throw anyone under the bus; and you don't publicly promote yourself at the expense of the team. Hope's comment derailed a team that had veered off track, and when the tournament was finally over I made a promise to myself: If I was ever forced to sit on the bench, for whatever reason, I would not react in a manner I'd regret later.

Once I was home in Hermosa Beach, down from the mountain and settling into the valley, depression crept back. "I'm the saddest person I have ever known," I texted to Are's mom, Dena. I fought to reconcile this feeling alongside my public and professional personality: fun, optimistic, motivational, driven. I felt a stubborn, secret gloom stalking me, finding me anywhere I turned. Yet I kept playing, and playing well. We matched up three times against Mexico in three different cities during our post–World Cup "celebration" tour in October. I started dating a new teammate, Megan Rapinoe, and as much as I liked her I was still fixated on Haley, and still wallowing in the old wounds she caused me.

A few weeks before Christmas, the team met in Los Angeles for a four-day camp. After the World Cup, Greg Ryan was fired, and we had a new coach, Pia Sundhage, a veteran soccer player who twice led the Swedish team to winning games in the World Cup, in 1991 and 1995. We also had new young players and a new veteran captain, 99er Christie Rampone—still known as "Pearcie" to us, after her maiden name. Pearcie and I had an agreement: She was the captain, the official face of the team, the wise and calm general who laid out the strategy before the war began. I was her obnoxious counterpart, the trusty lieutenant who led our team into battle.

A few of the veteran leaders, myself included, met privately with Pia to discuss what had happened at the World Cup. This team had a chemistry problem, we argued, and it was going to be a problem moving forward if we wanted to win games. Pia's answer was simple and left no room for debate: "Hope is the goalkeeper. You guys have to figure this out and deal with it."

When the rest of the team joined us, she pulled out a guitar and sang Bob Dylan in broken English: "For the times they are a-changin'." She was telling all of us to move past the World Cup disaster, but I took the words personally. The 2008 Olympics were fast approaching, and it was about time to emerge from my darkness, to peer out from the cave and find my other self.

Before I left, Pia asked to speak to me alone.

"Listen," she said, "I don't want you to have to worry about being a captain and dealing with that stuff. I want you to just worry about scoring goals."

"I'm fine with that," I assured her. "I want to worry about scoring goals, but I'm also still going to lead. So you're going to get, like, three birds with two stones."

I left camp feeling happier than I had in a year. Some disagreements lingered, but I knew we could overcome the World Cup drama. Together, we were the best in the world, and we all needed each other to win.

Once again I removed all bad habits from my life, instantly and easily. Sugar, fried food, junk television—anything that messed up my body or mind—ceased to exist in my life. Soon, my freakish internal scale readjusted its settings.

By July 16, five days before we left for Beijing, I was ready to steamroll my path to the goal. Injuries aside, I had never felt so fit and focused and certain of victory. That night we had an exhibition against Brazil, our last game before the Olympics began, and the team finally felt together, ready to play for another gold.

In the locker room, Pearcie motioned everyone to gather for our pregame talk. Her advice was practical and precise, spoken in the language all of us knew best: "We want to go out and really defend, and we want to switch the point of attack, but it doesn't mean we always have to go down the same side. We can continually switch the point, however long it takes for that moment to open up. Then, of course, we want to get in the box and throw numbers in the box and score goals."

Out on the field we got into our huddle, faces close and arms intertwined behind backs. It was my turn to speak.

"We have to go out and play for each other," I said. "If we're all on the same page we can play for each other. Every time you put this jersey on, it means something." My voice got louder. "We got this! We *got* this! We . . . we . . ." and my words tripped over each other, tumbling out in the wrong order and making no sense at all. "I'm such an idiot," I said, and everybody laughed. I understood, then, that we all needed to laugh; it was the only thing that muted the pregame tension. "Whatever," I added, slapping my forehead. "Pearcie!"

On cue, Pearcie thrust her hand into the middle of the circle, waiting for our hands to stack on top. "Oosa on three!" she called, our abbreviation for "USA." And we responded, all together: "Oosa, Oosa, Oosa, ah!"

The night air was hot, so hot I imagined steam hissing up from the field, marking the spots where my cleats stepped. We were hustling, cornering the Brazilians, cramping their style. At all times I was tuned in to where the ball was, and I was running as fast as I ever had, gaining speed. Cheers from the crowd rose up to follow me, and as I was about to make my move I was stopped by the point of my opponent's knee. It stabbed at my leg, hard. I fell to the ground and saw right away that my foot and my thigh were turned in opposite directions, as if in a disagreement that could never be resolved.

My mind delivered its diagnosis: Both the tibia and fibula—the two bones in my lower leg—were broken. Then I realized, suddenly: We were leaving for the Olympics in five days, and I was not going to be on that plane. Inside my head, depression took root. *Not now*, I thought, and shooed it away. I had to be on my game. I had to be a captain.

It was the worst physical pain I'd ever endured. Worse than my ankle, worse than my toe, worse than the gash in my scalp. Lying on the field, I thought of my parents, watching back home in Rochester, eagerly awaiting their trip to China for the Olympics. Over the years we'd created a system: If I was ever down, I'd give a thumbs-up so that they'd know I was okay. This time I left my thumb down, and instead called the trainers over.

Pearcie got there first.

"What happened?" she asked, squatting down.

"I broke my leg. My tib and fib are both broken."

"Are you sure?"

"Yeah," I said, and my mind went right back to the game. "Tell Pia to get a sub ready."

The emergency crew rolled a stretcher toward me. I felt them lift my body off the ground and carry me off the field. It was dark as the ambulance doors closed by my feet. My leg felt like a bomb had gone off inside it. Someone stabbed a needle into my arm, and the pain began to creep away, bit by bit.

"Can I borrow a phone?" I asked no one in

particular, and a medic brought one over. I dialed Lauren Cheney, a new teammate who also played forward. She hadn't made the Olympic roster a few weeks ago, but I thought she was up to the job.

"Cheney," I said, without even saying hello. "I hope you've been working out. I'm injured, and if they replace me with another forward it's going to be you."

She laughed. "Shut up, you're being dramatic. You're fine, you're always fine."

"I'm serious," I said again. "I can't run. So *you* need to go for a run and get fit, because you're going to the Olympics."

I hung up and called my parents. They were watching the game on television, and my mother already had plane reservations for the next flight out. The pain medicine crept farther into my bloodstream. "I want my mom," I whispered, hanging up, and the dial tone lulled me into a restless sleep.

LEADER

IT TOOK THE DOCTORS FOUR hours to piece me back together again. They created a patchwork of screws and inserted a titanium rod through my knee, piercing the bone marrow of the tibia, connecting the two broken halves. A few teammates were waiting in my hospital room when they wheeled me in after surgery. My eyes made out blurred features and distorted voices: Pearcie, Kate Margraff, Angela Hucles, Heather O'Reilly, Leslie Osborne. Others came and went as I drifted in and out. Someone brought me my phone and computer. I searched my name and "broken leg" and watch the resulting video clips, each showing my agony from a different angle.

"Can you please stop watching that?" someone

asked. She—I'm not quite sure who it was—meant well, but no, I couldn't stop; my brain demanded proof that I wasn't caught in some endless nightmare. "I just can't believe this happened," I heard myself say. "It's so weird. I don't get hurt. I can play through anything." Silently I continued the conversation: *I did everything right this time; I was prepared and centered and controlled.* And then came the silent response: *When are you going to learn you can't control everything?*

My mother arrived, and I wept again when I saw her. When my phone rang, my mother handed it to me. It was Megan Rapinoe, or Pinoe, my girlfriend and teammate, and my mother left the room to let me talk.

She asked how I was and told me she was so sorry. I knew she understood, having injured her knee badly enough to have missed the 2007 World Cup; she, too, was out for the Olympics. After a few moments of commiserating, she got to the point. "I can't do this," she confessed, as kindly as she could. She went on: "We keep getting injured. It's a sign we're not meant to be together. We need a break. I hope you understand."

I was crying again when my mother returned, and I calmed down just enough to tell her of our conversation. She sat on the edge of the bed, stroking my hair. "She doesn't deserve your tears," she said, proving that she, at least, had accepted what she couldn't control. She'd had a few lessons in that regard; my sister Laura had also come out as a lesbian.

I dozed off, then woke up. Dozed off, woke up, dozed off, woke up. After one interval, I asked my mother for my computer. Opening my email, I found a message from Haley and was suddenly and strangely alert:

> Abby, that did not look good. What happened to you just now? I just saw you say it was broken. You are a horse, a work horse, and I hope so much that this injury is not as bad as it seems.
>
> Your team and coaching staff looked shocked on TV. I could see the color leave their faces simultaneously. You have their respect and admiration, that is so evident. Their leader was leaving. I could see how much you bring to that team, and the respect those you lead have for you. You were brave, too, twenty times more calm than I was on the couch. You have so much support and love. I am so sorry for this. I am sick to my stomach and upset and I can imagine you're in shock. I am so sorry.
>
> Love,
> Haley

Immediately I opened a new message and began typing:

Hey, at the moment it's 4:10 a.m. on Friday. I can't sleep so I grabbed my computer and saw your email. Thanks for your words. They meant a lot. It was so weird because right when it happened I knew. I felt the bones snap. I saw exactly what you saw on television. So when everyone else was freaking out, I couldn't.

Hilarious that I was trying to lessen the blow for other people. Because honestly, it is okay. I am okay. My leg hurts like crazy and this situation stinks, but there are way worse things in life. And maybe I'm just in denial or something, but immediately I went to the positives and just focused on those. I am bummed for my teammates as I am kind of important for this team, so it's tough bearing this sort of responsibility for them, but it would be cool for them to overcome this and win it anyway. It would just be amazing to me.

I can't believe you still watch my games. I don't say that because I want you to confirm anything to me, just that I am surprised that you do. A few questions for you: How are you/what are you doing these days? I am going to have a lot more time on my hands these next few months. Any good ideas for me? Remember, I'll be on crutches so hiking and stuff will be out of the question.

I had a feeling a few weeks back that you're preggo. Could this be true? Or am I just nuts? Thanks for the email, Hal. It meant a lot. If you want, call. It would be nice to catch up. I felt the love you sent. Much appreciated. Sending mine back . . .

The hospital released me, sending me back to my Hermosa Beach condo, where Kara was waiting to take care of me. She'd replaced Are as my roommate after he moved back to Florida to start a personal training business. I was grateful; I needed her calm, sensible perspective. I returned to the hospital for rehab and was eager to start, if only to get back a sense of control.

At first we tried three hours per day, rotating my ankle, contracting my quad to fire up the muscle, which seemed to have shriveled up overnight. I limped up and down the hallways, a trainer on either side. I was in pain, constantly, but the team doctor told me I needed to accept the fact that this was going to hurt, and that it was going to take time, more time than I probably imagined, more time than I'd ever had to give anything else.

After the day's rehab, with nothing but time, I attempted to be a leader from 6,200 miles away. I contemplated flying to China to surprise my team, but during an acupuncture appointment, with needles sticking out of me from head to toe, I concluded that I'd only be a distraction. Instead, I decided to write them a letter, some words to inspire them before the games began.

I opened a new email and began:

To the U.S. Olympic Women's National Soccer Team:

I am hoping to somehow inspire you guys, and I thought my being there could do just that. But the truth is, I'm not the inspiration. It's the situation that's inspiring—and you do not in fact need me there.

I thought a lot about my injury, and what keeps coming up for me is that this has happened for a reason. It makes me realize that this team has to find its way without me. What's so amazing about this whole thing is that every one of you has the opportunity to truly become the best of champions. This is so fitting in terms of the way things have gone all year. I have done everything and then some that has been asked of me; you all have done everything and then some that has been asked of you. You have turned over every stone, and Pia is all about challenges. So why not embrace this one? Because the truth is that this challenge that's in front of you will in fact define this team. Not to stress you all out, but it gives me chilly bumps just thinking about it.

It's a simple question: How do you want this team to be remembered? And I know you're probably all really sick of getting questions about how things will turn out without me on the field. I'm sorry about that. I'm sure it's annoying, but really, it's a great question and I hope you all have talked about it, because it's going to be what everyone wants to see.

I can safely say that I have no doubt you all will rise to the occasion. No doubt at all, because that's what this team is, has, and will always be. It's timeless and no one person decides its fate. Do you all feel that? Do you all understand that? I feel like that was the lesson I really learned last year during the

World Cup. Obviously I didn't fully grasp it. I do now. I have been totally humbled by this whole thing and hope that you all have been, too. Things have changed, and you all need to believe that you can do this.

Look around the room. Look each other in the eyes. This is a team that will win gold, and you can't doubt that for one second. Yeah, you're going to make mistakes. Yes, you will be nervous. Yes, goals may get scored. It's not about what happens; it's about how you react to all of it. If you let doubt seep in for just a moment then you won't succeed. I promise you that. So if you make a bad pass or you miss an open girl or you can't find anything good about your game, just look around. Look where you are. See that you're playing not to win, but you're playing to define yourself.

You are playing to make your mark on this game. It's honor that you're in search of, and if you stop thinking so hard about success or failure and instead focus on each other, you will find way more than honor. You will find the purest part of what makes all of this so special.

I have felt that once before—four years

ago, at our last Olympics. Some of you haven't ever felt it. Some have felt it more than me. But this will be different from anything else you've ever experienced before. I just know it. Can you? Do you feel what an opportunity this is? Are you in control of how it plays out? You all have a choice. Are you going to cry into a corner or will you stand up and fight? What are you willing to give? Because it takes more than what you think you're even capable of. But that's what these kinds of tournaments are about. The team that's standing on top of the tallest podium will have gone past their own limitations. They will have believed in each other 100% of the time. They will have enjoyed the process. They will have overcome problems, and most importantly the team that is standing on the podium getting the gold medal wrapped around their necks will have done it together.

I believe in my heart that every one of you can and will make that commitment to one another, that no matter what, you will do whatever it takes to experience that moment together. It will be supreme and I would love nothing more than to see that happen. I hope you all feel that you are ready for that.

By the time I typed that last period, I was sweating and slightly out of breath. I wasn't finished, though, and my fingers started tapping again; I wanted to address each teammate personally, one by one.

I told Nicole Barnhart that while we all mercilessly mocked her compression socks, she was clearly the toughest chick on the team.

I told Heather Mitts what I'd been thinking since our days in college—she had the best legs I'd ever seen—and that she was the most consistent player. Plus, she never let me beat her during drills, and that made me crazy.

I told Pearcie what she already knew: She'd been my rock the past few years. She was solid, loyal, kind, strong, stubborn, and kept secrets better than anyone I know.

I marveled at Rachel Buehler's fearlessness. I congratulated Lindsay Tarpley for her impeccable work ethic. I told Natasha Kai that her passion was inspiring. I admired Shannon Boxx's willingness to attack every opportunity. I thanked Amy Rodriguez for putting up with my lengthy thoughts when we roomed together the previous year in China. I praised Heather O'Reilly's huge heart and six-pack abs. I got philosophical on Aly Wagner and told her, "Your being is special." I called Carli Lloyd the most gifted player I'd ever known, and criticized anyone who dismissed her just because she grew up in New Jersey.

I noted that Tobin Heath was wise beyond her years, and the most "going-the-full" person in history. I acknowledged Stephanie Cox's willingness to have uncomfortable conversations. I called Kate Markgraf the most underrated player in the history of this national team. I appreciated that Angela Hucles had a perspective on life that was so perfectly and uniquely her own. I told Lori Chalupny—"Chupes"— that she always brought two words to mind: most solid. I was blown away by Briana Scurry's strength, and I asked her to share her valuable secrets with all of us.

I thanked Lauren Cheney for stepping in to replace me, and told her it was her time now—her turn. I apologized to Hope Solo, admitting that our World Cup disaster forced me to do some soul-searching. Instead of being honest and compassionate, I had been controlling and manipulative. And in moving forward, I promised to get past my own ego and learn to trust. I told her not to be afraid to show the world her softer side. I knew it was there, I said, because I'd seen it.

By then I was crying again, and in pain, and the laptop lay hot across my thighs. My stiff fingers pushed to conclude:

"So that's it," I wrote. "I'm sorry this has been so

long, but it's important for me to express my thoughts clearly, and I know I even failed at that. I guess I've said it all. I love you all so much and I'm so sorry I'm not there with you physically. I am with you, though. If you make a mistake or you're scared or you don't know what to do, just know that I am with you. Just feel me by your side. I am there. Open your hearts and you'll know. If you do, you will be champions. But it has to be a commitment from everyone. You can do this. You can win. I just know it. Good luck and play your hearts out. I'll be watching."

I was watching from my couch when we played Norway on August 6. We looked lost out there, timid and deflated, and I screamed at the TV: "No—what are you doing? Get on your mark! Move, move!" My tirade woke up my neighbor all the way from across the street. *Who cares?* I thought. *I'm going to be as loud as I want.* My boisterous armchair coaching had no effect, and we lost 2–0.

I slept off my sorrow.

We had better luck in the next few rounds, beating Japan, New Zealand, and Canada. In the semifinals we faced Japan again, and for this game I flew out to New York, crutching my way through the airport and cringing at the turbulence. When I landed, Are was there to greet me; he flew up from Florida so we could watch the game together. We drove upstate to the Thousand Islands, a cluster of islands on the United States–Canadian border, where my parents owned a plot of land and a secluded, ancient house. We cheered together as the team won, 4–2.

For the gold medal game against Brazil, we decided to watch at a local diner. As soon as they opened we slid into booths, with me on the end so I could stretch my leg and shake my crutch at the screen. I was too nervous to eat breakfast, and my omelet congealed on its plate as I watched Marta, Brazil's formidable and flashy leader, twist and spin her way across the field, looking more like a samba dancer than a forward—"Pelé with skirts," they called her, a nickname reportedly given to her by Pelé himself. In the eighteenth minute Pearcie shut her down, but Marta again found her rhythm, veering around our defenders, pulling back her leg, and releasing it square into the ball—a beautiful shot, I had to admit—and my breath stopped in the back of my throat. . . . *It's wide! A miss!* I exhaled.

The Brazilians excelled at the art of drawing fouls; one mild collision and their players flung themselves to the ground, flailing and rolling around like they were on fire. A Brazilian named Formiga tried this trick after colliding with Heather Mitts in the thirty-seventh minute, but thankfully the referee wasn't impressed. At halftime both sides were still scoreless, and the diner was filling up with patrons, some of whom recognized me and strolled over to wish me well. It was the first time all day I'd felt a pinch of sadness, and I told myself to remember the words I wrote to my team: *You do not need me there.*

Early in the second half we looked bewildered and clumsy, out of step and offbeat, and we were forced to play defense, cornering Marta and preventing her advance. She found an opening anyway, kicking the ball toward our goal, blocked by Hope in the nick of time. Seven minutes left in regular time and we were suddenly commanding the action: a rocket by Carli (wide!); a shot by Angela Hucles (short!); and another by Amy Rodriguez that landed in their goalie's gloves. The clock dwindled to zero: We were heading into overtime.

Seven minutes in, Carli fired one off, and their goalie dove a bit short—goal! Twenty-three minutes to gold. I watched through my fingers. Both sides were playing a game of tag, back and forth, back and forth, and despite the Brazilians' furious shooting, nothing found the net. It was over and we won. *We won.* The diner patrons clapped and shouted, and I hopped happily on my good leg. I switched to my bad one, craving the physical pain—anything to distract from the sad rage of not being there on the field.

My phone buzzed. It was Dez, our equipment manager, calling from the locker room. "Hold on," he instructed, and I heard a roaring rush of screams and cheers, a celebration I was missing. I listened until I couldn't stand the sound anymore; I so badly wished my voice were in that chorus.

I hung up, terrified that they'd won without me.

APPRENTICE

IN THE WEEKS FOLLOWING THE Olympics, I existed on two settings: numbed and tortured. Kara arranged an intense regimen of ice and elevation and compression, which I was convinced would help me heal. She slept on the couch with me, her head by my feet, and a few times per night I accidentally woke her up with a swift kick to the temple. Without complaint, she rose and wrapped me in fresh ice. Occasionally, I crept back toward consciousness, coherent enough to drag my laptop toward me and power it on. I went online and bought a guitar, which became a new obsession, a way to channel my energy with my fingers instead of my feet. Sometimes, when I was lucky,

I slept through the night, and for those few hours my mind let me believe it wasn't all just a terrible dream.

I temporarily shed my fear of crying, allowing myself to sob openly and without hesitation, at least from the safety of my couch. These jags were about more than missing the Olympics; they were about my relationship with soccer, which, in a way, meant they were about my relationship with myself. With past defeats I insisted on accepting all the blame: I wasn't fit enough; I wasn't prepared enough; I didn't want it enough, or I wanted other things more. For this Olympics, for the first time in my life, I didn't believe those reasons. For the first time in my life I believed that soccer betrayed me, and I wanted to know why.

I was never good at soul-searching, having spent my entire twenty-eight years focusing outward, throwing my energy into the air and seeing where it stuck. I wasn't sure where or how to start. Kara helped, burning incense and talking me through the basics of meditation. I tried, feeling awkward and embarrassed, as if I was on a first date with someone too good for me. I couldn't make my mind shut up; it was just as loud and obnoxious as my mouth. Kara told me this was normal; the wandering mind was digging up all the negativity and yanking it out.

When I wasn't sitting perfectly still, working out my brain, I was at physical therapy, finding my way back to my body. I was soft and lopsided and every step shot a bolt of lightning through my bones. My doctor predicted my recovery would take a year, and mentally I chopped that time in half: *Six months, max.* Every quad extension was as rigorous and painful as a dozen successive suicide runs. I pushed, added more weight, stretched, balanced, walked, stepped, iced, compressed, and repeated, willing the muscle back to life. I imagined myself returning to the field, sprinting its length, practicing plays, feeling my head against the ball. Soccer proved, to my surprise, that I was breakable, and I decided I'd find every piece I lost along the way.

At the end of September, I was well enough to travel to Manhattan for the draft of a new professional soccer league, Women's Professional Soccer, or WPS, scheduled to launch in the spring. The league's organizers were optimistic about its success, and I planned to play for the Washington Freedom, my old club team. A reporter for the *New York Times* asked me about missing the Olympics, and I reached for one of my new Zen mantras: "I wasn't devastated," I said, "because I accepted it when it happened. I try to live in the present."

In the first weeks of 2009, I packed up and headed back east to Washington, DC.

On March 1, the first day of our preseason, I was in the locker room with my teammates, getting ready for practice. Some were old friends, like Briana Scurry and Lori Lindsey, but there were new faces, too, including a woman named Sarah Huffman. I was immediately attracted to her.

At practice, I was constantly aware of where she was standing, and I maneuvered myself to be next to her in drills. I was nearby when she twisted her leg awkwardly on the turf and went down, flatly and swiftly, as if yanked by some unseen hand. She was wincing, holding her right knee, and when her eyes opened they met mine. I was standing over her, absolutely still, holding her gaze.

"You're going to be okay," I said, in the calmest tone I'd ever used. "You don't know what's wrong. You don't know what you've done. You have to wait for the MRI. Just take this one step at a time, and believe me when I say you're going to be okay."

A few hours later the team heard the diagnosis: a torn ACL. That night, I planned to stop by her house. I assembled a care package, including DVDs, a book, and a handwritten note telling her how sorry I was, and that I knew exactly how she was feeling. When I arrived, she had her leg up and was surrounded by some of our teammates. She loved the package and my note, and we all watched some TV. I sat as close to Sarah as I could and did my best to make her laugh. Over the next few days we exchanged long emails about injuries, and the lack of control that accompanies them. I nearly begged: *Please tell me what I can do to help you get to the other side.*

I had a chance a few days later on March 5, Sarah's birthday. We had off from practice the next morning, so a group of us went out to celebrate. When she said she had to go to the bathroom, I helped her up from her chair, and when she came back to the table she grabbed my hand, lacing her fingers through mine. I looked at her, tightened my grip, but failed to make a move.

By the time she had her surgery, I was spending more time at her place than my own. I made her coffee, fetched her books, perched trays of food on her chest. I kept her company while she lay on the couch, her leg in a device that moved it automatically, bending and straightening. Her mom came to visit, and she left us alone for long stretches so we could talk privately. Sarah opened her eyes as I squeezed in next to her.

"Do you want to be girlfriends with me?" she asked.

"Yeah, I do," I said.

Within the week I knew that if I could marry her, I would.

HEAD CASE

THE YEARS 2009 AND 2010 were full of both good and bad memories. In the summer of 2009, exactly one year and three days after I broke my leg, we played a friendly game against Canada. The match was in Rochester and my entire family was among the 8,500 fans. Sarah surprised me by showing up, waving at me from the stands. It was the first time she'd be meeting my family, and I was sure they'd love her as much as I did. We were tied, 0–0, and in the seventy-eighth minute I saw my chance, pushing the ball past the right leg of the Canadian goalkeeper and into the net. It was my one hundredth career goal and the crowd erupted, their cheers lifting me up, taking away some of the misery of the previous year.

"I can't really describe the emotion," I said after the game, my nieces and nephews lining up to hug me. "It's been a long year, and to come home to score the hundredth goal in Rochester couldn't be more of a picture-perfect ending."

I remember a Washington Freedom game against the Boston Breakers in May 2010, an unremarkable, 0–0 matchup except for one spectacular collision: My nose hit the opposing goalkeeper's arm. I heard a crack and felt the bone and cartilage slide across my face, ending up in the middle of my left cheek. It was so disgusting my teammates looked away. When I had the gauze removed, Sarah—who had a lifelong fear of blood—was by my side, rocking back and forth, hands over her eyes so she didn't faint from the sight.

I remember when the national team faltered, losing to Mexico and facing the possibility of not qualifying for the 2011 World Cup in Germany. It was unbelievable that we lost to Mexico—our total score against them in past games was 106–9—and even more unthinkable that we might be excluded from a major tournament. In order to get back on track, we had to beat Costa Rica, and we did, 3–0. I scored two of those goals, despite a deep gash along my forehead, yet we still weren't in the clear: We had to beat Italy in the playoff series. Losing meant we'd be staying home.

I remember the media attention surrounding our potential defeat and humiliation, and how it felt so unfair. I took the opportunity to share my observations with the *New York Times*. "The irony of the whole thing," I said, "is that when the US men win, they get the coverage, but when the US women lose, we get the coverage. . . . The joke among us is that we planned it this way and that we knew this was the only way to get the coverage we think we deserve." I tucked this feeling away to look at it later, knowing it was bigger than just the tone of newspaper articles. This discrimination affected every aspect of our game.

I remember when Women's Professional Soccer began sinking, once again failing to re-create the buzz and excitement that follow World Cup and Olympic years. Teams lost millions of dollars and began dropping out, one by one. Toward the end of 2010, the Washington Freedom's owners sold the team to a Boca Raton–based businessman named Dan Borislow, who renamed it "magicJack" after one of his products. He recruited me and a few other high-profile members of the national team: Hope Solo, Pearcie, Shannon Boxx. Sarah joined, too, and we moved together to Florida.

I liked Dan, and the feeling was mutual; he saw

himself in me—loud and never shy. I admired his willingness to say what others were thinking, his trust in his own instincts. He had a bold, modern attitude toward women's soccer. In emails to *ESPN The Magazine*, he said things I didn't yet have the courage to discuss out loud. "Why is it okay that the athletes who represent our country the best should be paid wages that leave them at the poverty level?" he asked. "I would never pay someone who is best in their field these types of ridiculous wages. It would be embarrassing. We should not have a pro league in this country unless they get paid real money." He acted on this, giving each of us a significant raise, and announced, "It is not okay to treat women badly. . . . The women to a large degree have accepted this treatment."

I remember going back to Los Angeles in the off-season, bringing Sarah with me, double-dating with Kara and her girlfriend. Sarah was completely in my life, with me through all the highs and lows of 2009 and 2010. In 2011, I'd need her more than ever.

GOAT

THE COUNTDOWN TO THE 2011 World Cup wasn't easy. Every day, bit by bit, my body was becoming a lesser version of itself. Every part of it had to be addressed and dealt with before I made it to the field. My shaky ankle required wrapping, and my Achilles tendon needed two kinds of treatments that were so long and intense I thought my body would never be the same. At night I wore a support on my foot, and in the morning I needed to work out my ankle for a half hour just to be able to stand. I alternated between wearing cleats and a boot to keep my ankle in a set position. My leg bones could feel the rain before it fell. I was newly thirty-one, and for the first time wondering how much longer I could play soccer.

But at the World Cup in Germany, I had to talk myself through the pain and push it off to the sidelines. I began the tournament in a scoring drought, kicks deflecting off the post and headers veering wide, an embarrassment made bigger by my teammates' unspoken concern: *What's wrong with Wambach?* During our final group match game against Sweden, the ball soared toward me and I fought for position. Planting my legs, I reared my torso back like a slingshot, snapped forward, and connected with the knob of my shoulder, shoving it in for a goal. *Nothing's wrong with Wambach*, I thought. *I'm back, at least for now.*

We moved on to face Brazil in the quarterfinals. I recalled how the Brazilians not only beat us in 2007, but danced and sang in our hotel lobby as we entered, heartbroken. There was a chance the scene could be repeated—we were again staying in the same hotel as them—and I gathered the younger players around to tell them the story. "I would give up every goal I've ever scored to win this World Cup," I said. "You have to be willing to give up everything." Silently I added: *I'd give up everything because this might be the last World Cup I ever see.*

From the field, the spectators seemed tiny. My parents, siblings, Are, Dena, Kara, and Sarah sat among thousands of people eager for us to lose. The July heat hung heavy and low, making me sweat before I even started to move. Seventy-four seconds in and we were on the board, accidentally, when Brazilian defender Daiane deflected the ball into her own net. Ugly, but I'd take it. There was a chorus of long and lusty boos; no one liked Americans.

I got my first shot, crowding the Brazilian goalkeeper inside the box, but it swerved wide. Twelve minutes later Brazil came to life, with Marta prancing fifty yards down the field and taking a shot. It arced high, too high, and they remained scoreless. The crowd swelled into a wave, standing and tossing their hands, hoping to fuel Brazil's momentum.

We went back and forth, up and down, until suddenly I was airborne, a body on top of me, collapsing into a tangle of arms and legs as we slammed into the ground. I twisted my head to see the Brazilian defender Aline. She got a booking—a warning from the referee—for the tackle, and then Marta earned one by arguing with the referee about it. By halftime we were still up, 1–0. Beneath the wrappings, my body and mind were both screaming.

Pearcie and Pia did their usual thing in the locker room, giving us strategy and wisdom, and then I did mine in the huddle: patriotism, togetherness, grit, and a few jokes. On the count of three, we chanted,

"Oosa, Oosa, Oosa, ah!" and we were back on the field.

In the sixty-fifth minute, Rachel Buehler leaped sideways at Marta, taking her down, with the Brazilian performing her usual theatrics, flipping and somersaulting. It worked. Rachel got a red card—she was out of the game—and Brazil was going to get a penalty kick. Later, Rachel told me she watched the game on TV, crying the whole time, sure she had lost it for us. For the duration of the game we had just ten players on the field.

The Brazilian player Cristiane lined up to take the penalty kick, but Hope pitched herself in its path and stopped it. Then the referee made an insane call, claiming Hope moved off her line, and ordered a do-over. This time, Marta stepped up. She kicked one way while Hope jumped the other, and the game was tied, 1–1. The crowd turned, booing the referees and scowling at the Brazilians, and we became the good guys, the underdogs. Chants of *USA! USA!* filtered down to the field. By the end of regulation, the game was still tied. We were going into overtime.

In the ninety-second minute, Marta scored on a set play at such a severe angle that I couldn't help but admire the shot. Brazil took the lead. *That's going to be that*, I thought. *That's how soccer goes. If you score in overtime, that's usually the game. We're still down a man, and everything is against us.* Then my heart responded to my mind, protesting: *No! We can still do this. It's not over yet.*

We had to keep playing, regardless, acting as though we believed we had a chance. We hustled, we took our spots, we tried to execute a set play and failed. Wasted moves, wasted energy. I was heaving, running as hard as I ever had and not quite getting where I needed to be. I wanted to do anything to get closer to the goal. I reached it, finally, and managed a weak kick that skidded low and around the pole, then was stopped in the nick of time by their keeper.

I was getting angry. I wanted the ball to go where I wanted it to go; I wanted my body to do what it was being asked. I wanted this to be as effortless for me as it had always been. And just like that, my body talked back, louder than I'd ever heard it speak: *Make me. I dare you.*

I accepted the challenge—I'd never known how to turn one down—and screamed to my teammates: "If we just get one chance, I know we'll score!"

Marta seemed to be in three places at once, sailing and swooping. We were stretched thin and exhausted, and time was dwindling: 113 minutes, 118, 120. The final whistle could blow any second. Brazil's Erika went down, writhing in pain over an invisible tackle, a classic plot to run down the clock. A stretcher was called for, and she hopped on and off it, miraculously ready to play again. Another waterfall of boos came from the crowd. But her theatrics helped, giving us time to move the ball forward.

We were ping-ponging it across and up the field: Pearcie to Ali Krieger to Carli Lloyd, who took a bunch of touches. *What are you doing?* I thought, and yelled, "Carli, play direct! Don't kick it wide!" My ear was anticipating the sound of the whistle, signaling our loss, our time to pack up and go home. Carli played the ball to Pinoe, my ex and now close friend. I wasn't sure if she saw me, but she was running toward me, taking a touch, and I knew exactly what she'd do next: look up and bomb it into the box. She did, the ball flying from her toe into a magnificent arc, stretching higher and higher . . .

I crept into position, waiting to pounce. My mind gave me a last-second pep talk: *Please don't miss. It would be the most epic failure in the history of the game if you miss.*

The memory of every past goal was packed into that second, informing the way I moved—leaping off my right leg, slanting shoulders forward, matching the ball to my hairline, a puzzle piece finding its slot. That sweet, familiar second of darkness.

I opened my eyes and knew: I didn't miss. It was the latest goal ever scored in the World Cup.

I celebrated just like any Brazilian would, running toward my teammates and sliding on the turf, stopping myself just before I reached cement. When I jumped up they were all around me, bouncing and slapping my back. Pinoe leaped into my arms and I carried her for a few steps. It wasn't over, but we were close. *We got this*, I thought, and we did: Five penalty kicks later, the board was lit with the final score: USA: 5, Brazil: 3.

We won the battle but lost the war, falling in the final to Japan, which was still recovering from that spring's earthquake and tsunami; I reasoned that their country needed the win more than ours did. I also took the loss as a personal message: Soccer still supported me in a way nothing else did, and we were not yet finished with each other.

ROMANTIC

DESPITE OUR SECOND-PLACE FINISH AT the World Cup, America's interest in soccer surged to a degree unseen since the era of the 99ers. I celebrated the postgame reports describing celebrities' reactions to our win over Brazil. "Wambach!!!!" comedian Seth Meyers tweeted after my late goal. "Wowwwwww! Goal was amazing," added NFL star Kerry Rhodes. LeBron James, P. Diddy, and Gabrielle Union all chimed in with their compliments and congratulations. The team was invited to appear on the *Today* show, *Good Morning America*, and *The Late Show with David Letterman*.

For me, the most meaningful words came from

Mia Hamm. "How did you do that?" she asked. "That was the most amazing thing I've ever witnessed." Dan Borislow, who watched from the stands, echoed that response, telling me it was the "most impressive athletic play to ever happen in the history of women's soccer." Random people told me they remembered exactly where they were when they saw my goal. Endorsement offers came from Gatorade, Nike, and Panasonic. I sensed a turning point for soccer; maybe the women's game would now find the attention and respect it deserved.

When I returned to Florida, I was met with a hard dose of reality: My magicJack club team was about to fall apart. While the national players were in Germany, the rest of the team filed a complaint against Dan Borislow. After a loss to Boston, Dan sent an almost cruel email: "I didn't play this terrible game, you did." He also threatened them with "suicide runs"—a mile in only five minutes—and insisted they take scalding Jacuzzi baths before practice. My old teammate Briana Scurry quit. While the WPS investigated the grievance, Dan was banned from the sidelines, and I was named the player-coach.

Attendance in the beginning of the season was awful, rarely more than one thousand spectators. After the World Cup, the numbers increased, and the high was a crowd of 15,404 when we headed north to play the Western New York Flash at their home stadium—*my* home stadium, with my family filling rows and rows of bleachers. It was a single-game attendance record for the league, and I addressed the cheering crowd at halftime, apologizing for being on the bench because of my Achilles tendon. They chanted my name and waved Abby bobbleheads. Our season ended the following month after a playoff loss to Philadelphia, and even with the new enthusiasm in soccer, I worried about the future of the league—especially when the WPS board of directors, naming ongoing issues with Dan, voted to terminate the magicJack team.

In the fall, Sarah and I moved back to Hermosa Beach and I started to plan my proposal. Our similarities brought us together, but I thought our differences would make us last. We each knew our roles and played them well. I cooked, piling the counters with pots and pans, and she cleaned, wiping up every last crumb. I loved to shop and she waited for sales. I scattered and she organized. She was passionate but even-tempered and was never afraid to challenge me. I was happy, happier than I've ever been, which gave me a new appreciation for those long periods of depression. Without them, the happiness would be duller.

I had a ring designed by my family's jeweler in Rochester, and the end result was perfect: a cushion-cut diamond surrounded by smaller stones, set in platinum. While I was at it, I ordered two wedding rings for Sarah, simple bands of round diamonds. Put together, it looked like the center stone was floating on a sparkling pillow of diamonds. I decided to pop the question around the holidays. I planned each moment and daydreamed about how it would unfold.

For Christmas, we flew to Dallas to visit her parents. I was very traditional in some ways; there were lessons from my mother I couldn't unlearn. I would never get a tattoo, and I didn't want my partner to have one. I would never find out the sex of my children before they were born. And I believed that if you wanted to propose, it was respectful to ask your partner's parents for their blessing. In Dallas, I knew it was my only chance, and I was so nervous. After dinner, I found them in the kitchen. The three of us were alone; Sarah had gone out with her sister. Her mother was gathering plates and her father was washing dishes, hands plunged into the sink.

Pulling the ring out of my pocket, I said the words I'd been practicing in my head: I was in love with their daughter, and I wanted nothing more than to spend the rest of my life with her. I would honor and cherish her always, and take care of her, and it would mean everything if I could have their blessing.

Time passed. It could have been a minute, five, ten; I was too scared to count. Everyone was on pause. Me, standing with the ring pinched between my fingers. Sarah's mother, halfway to the sink, balancing a pyramid of plates. Her father, hands motionless beneath running water. *Drip, drip, drip.*

At last, her mother broke the silence. "Oh, wow," she said, and the words shook her dad into action. "Oh, wow," he repeated, and added, "I was not expecting that question."

I smiled, but I was shrinking inside. My mind looked for ways to justify his reaction. I knew her father worried that Sarah was in my shadow, soccer-wise, and he (understandably) wanted her to feel independent and be able to support herself. And while I knew it wasn't about *me*—her parents had always loved me—I suspected they'd hoped that Sarah's bisexuality meant that she might end up with a man. There was no denying it would be an easier life, but, I argued silently, not necessarily a happier one.

Finally, her mother spoke again. "Oh, we're so

thrilled!" she exclaimed, and rushed to hug me. I loved her even more for lying just to make me comfortable.

The day after Christmas, it was time to launch Phase II, which I'd been planning for months. I'd arranged for a group of our closest friends to meet in Breckenridge, Colorado, for New Year's. We'd rented a huge cabin set high in the mountains, and Sarah and I were there to greet each visitor. There was plenty of food to eat, and we hiked every morning. While Sarah was getting ready, I gathered all our friends and whispered my instructions. "Listen," I said. "At some point on this hike, when we come to a really steep hill, just stop and say, 'Hey, I'm tired. I'm going to go back.' And one by one you guys will walk down. And when we get back, we're going to have a huge engagement party." They agreed, and we headed out.

Breckenridge is 9,600 feet above sea level, and within twenty minutes all of us were gasping, our breath turning into smoke against the cold air. One by one our friends said they were exhausted, turned around, and headed back down to the cabin, until Sarah and I were alone at the top of a hill.

From my backpack I pulled out a photo album titled "Life As We Knew It." Every picture I'd taken of us since the beginning of our relationship was arranged in careful order, accompanied by funny or sentimental or romantic captions. The last page read: "I just have one more question." When she turned around I was on bended knee, holding the ring up.

I told her all the reasons I wanted to marry her.

She said yes.

HERO

BEFORE I CAME OUT OF hibernation for the Olympics, before Intense Abby stepped forward and asserted herself, Sarah told me she had a surprise.

"Hey," she said. "April 8 is the third anniversary of our first date. We're going somewhere."

We drove my Jeep twenty minutes from Hermosa to Long Beach, the wind cooling our faces as quickly as the sun warmed them, everything in harmony. She'd packed a picnic basket, but I wasn't allowed to peek inside. I attempted to guess our destination and she smiled in response. We pulled into a heliport, where a two-seater helicopter was waiting, and the pilot lifted us up and landed us in Catalina.

Taking my hand, she led me to a golf cart and we

drove around town, through the narrow streets, and stopped at a piece of land overlooking the ocean. She spread out a blanket and arranged our picnic: fruit and cheese. Then she retrieved a wooden box and instructed me to open it. I did and found a series of letter blocks, arranged in a sentence: WILL YOU MARRY ME? I looked up, shocked, and saw she was holding a ring: a thick platinum band filled inside with diamonds, exactly what I'd always wanted.

As we embraced a thought occurred to me, and I had to voice it: "Did you ask my mom and dad?"

"Yeah," she said, and took me through the moment. After I'd proposed at Christmas, she'd called my parents in New York and said she had a question to ask relating to Abby, to our relationship. She knew the question would make my parents uncomfortable and she began crying and fumbling her words, until my mother took pity and spoke first. "Don't cry," she said. "We love you, and as long as you're happy and as long as it's something Abby wants, we want you both to be happy."

I was happy—as happy about my mother's approval as I was about the proposal—and I settled into the moment, wishing I could stretch it into the future, with a guarantee it would never change.

* * *

After that trip, I met the national team for training camp in Florida. I was motivated, fully aware that this might be my last Olympics, and despite its age and ailments my body still did what I asked of it, falling back into its familiar routine:

First, I'd get up at 8 a.m. and immediately pee into a cup to check hydration levels. If my number was above 700, I had to address the fact that I was not yet equipped to play. Dawn Scott, our strength and conditioning coach, then calculated how many hydrating solutions I needed, and I got down to the business of drinking them as quickly as I could. More than sprints, more than weights, more than dieting, more than ninety minutes of nonstop scrimmaging, I hated drinking water. In fact, I listed it as one of my personal weaknesses, deserving of a proper title: "Terrible Drinker of Water." But I'd drink it down anyway.

Next, I'd eat breakfast (two fried eggs, hot sauce, toast) and drink coffee, undoing the hard work I'd done to hydrate. I'd read the paper, do a crossword puzzle. Tape my ankle and pull on my boot—my Achilles tendon was still in agony—and head to the field, slipping on my cleats as soon as I arrived. I'd start warm-up laps, jogging back and forth across the field, catching up with my teammates. What did they do the night before? What were they reading? What TV show were they watching? If I was feeling especially chatty, or if the collective mood was subdued, I'd say something shocking to shake things up.

Then it was on to drills, set plays, batting the ball with my head, over and over again. We'd hit the weight room for supersets and plyometrics. Afterward, I'd worry about increasing the size of my legs. Like every other girl on the planet, I've studied my body in the mirror and thought, *My thighs are huge.*

On to the recovery room, finally, where I'd pull on compression pants and sit still for a half hour, waiting for the swelling to deflate. To unwind, I'd play video games—soccer, football, and poker—and then call Sarah. I wanted to hear about her day and imagine I was there. *Four more months until the Olympics,* I told myself, *and then I can get back to my life.*

Finally, we headed to England, to the Olympics, a place I hadn't been to for eight years. I remembered how miserable I'd been back in 2008, laid up with my broken leg, having to summon every last leadership instinct to stop myself from flying to China—to stop myself from making it all about me. I was feeling strong and ready and, most of all, *present*, all my focus and energy on the task ahead. Before the flight, a reporter asked me what my expectations were for the Games.

"Based on the fact that we have so many fans now, and so many people pulling for us," I said, "for me, it's gold or bust."

My agent, Dan, was standing beside me. "Did you really just say that?" he asked.

"Sure did."

He laughed. "Well, you'd better win that gold, then."

"I got this," I told him. "We got this."

On the field against France, I could see that we did. Although we started off tentative and shaky, allowing two goals in the first sixteen minutes, we pushed back, finding our groove. I scored the first goal of the game: a corner kick from Pinoe that bounced perfectly off my head. Three more goals—one from Alex Morgan, and two from Carli—and we won our first game, 4–2. We won our second, too, against Colombia, where I got punched in my right eye; afterward I tweeted a close-up picture of it: "Thanks for all the well wishes. Eye is healing fine. #reversesmokeyeye #notcool."

We won next against North Korea—my busted eye didn't prevent me from scoring the game's only goal—and nine of my teammates dropped to the turf and celebrated by doing the "worm," the old-school dance move. We won another against New Zealand, with a goal from me and one from Sydney Leroux, who I'd started to mentor. She wore an expression of joyous shock, as if she couldn't quite believe what she'd done, and I recognized what I'd never had: a pure love for the game, so real and intense she'd even play alone.

Our semifinal game against Canada was later named by the *Globe and Mail* as "the greatest game of women's soccer ever played." The match was rough and dirty before it even began; John Herdman, Canada's head coach, accused us of "illegal tactics" and singled me out specifically, pointing to my header against France off a corner kick. I recognized what he was doing; he wanted to gain an early advantage by shaking our confidence and influencing the referees. Despite myself I had to admire him; I understood his willingness to do whatever it took to win.

From the opening whistle, the play was a brutal spectacle of tackles, shirt pulling, elbowing, jostling, and one deliberate stomp on Carli's head. The crowd booed Tobin Heath when she (fairly) won a battle. I was keeping my eye on Christine Sinclair, a forward who was neck and neck with me in the race to score the most international goals; as of that moment, she had 140 to my 142. I'd called her "the most underrated player on the planet," and in the twenty-third minute she proved it, spinning and twisting through our back line and finding herself free in the box. She curled a shot to Hope Solo's right and hit the net with conviction (141 to my 142 now) giving the Canadians momentum as we made our way toward halftime. We hadn't lost to Canada in eleven years, and I didn't intend to let them break that streak.

My body did what it does best, beating and blocking and barreling through. On a header attempt I was called for climbing, and the Canadian goalie blocked me anyway. Two minutes later I tried again, leaping high and forward and aiming my head at the ball, which soared just past the post. At halftime, it was still 1–0, and we gathered in the locker room and reiterated a team vow: "There is no way we're losing to Canada. There is no way we're going home without making it to the final and winning gold."

The second half started off as wild as the first, with frantic back-and-forth in the midfield and jostling in the box, elbows stabbing and hands pulling and heads banging. I launched myself upward, slamming the ball high with my chest—too high, it turned out, and I watched it vault over the bar. We executed set piece after set piece, but the Canadians had studied me, anticipating my every move. Sometimes, I just couldn't reach the goal; the box was far away. Pinoe was luckier, or maybe the Canadians just hadn't been paying attention to her, and she scored with a gorgeous corner kick in the fifty-third minute. We were tied, 1–1, and the play on both sides accelerated, the ball zigzagging up and down the field; in six wild minutes three goals were scored—another by Sinclair (142 to 142 now) and another by Pinoe and yet another by Sinclair; I cared less about her temporary lead in our goal race than I did about the Canadians' lead in the game, 3–2.

With seventeen minutes left, I noticed their goalkeeper trying to stall, taking longer than the allowed six seconds to dropkick the ball back into play. Within earshot of the referee, I started counting, making it all the way to ten. The referee noticed but did nothing. When their goalkeeper stalled again, I resumed my counting: "One, two, three . . ." and the referee blew her whistle for a six-second violation—an unusual, very rarely made call. I took a penalty kick, tying the game at 3–3. In the 123rd minute, Carli passed to Heather O'Reilly, who passed to Alex; she rocketed up and batted her head against the ball, sending it high over her defender and into the net.

We won, 4–3, and I found Alex in the pile of teammates. "I love you," I screamed at her. "I think I'm in love with you in this moment."

Meanwhile, Twitter blew up, condemning me for counting near the referee.

"Dear FIFA," read one tweet, "please investigate Abby Wambach for unsporting behaviour in attempting to influence the referee's decision."

Another: "Sorry, I will not be moved on this: Abby Wambach should be ashamed. It's the Olympics, remember."

And my personal favorite: "I want to get a punching bag, paste Abby Wambach's face on it, and work out."

I told reporters I regretted nothing: "You can say it's gamesmanship, you can say it's smart, but I'm a competitor. We needed to get a goal." Besides, I added, the incident rallied Canadians behind their team, and women's sports needed as much support as they could get, no matter the source or reason.

On August 8, a few hours before we were to meet Japan in the gold medal game, I opened my email and found a message from my friend Kara. I was so relieved to see it; we'd had a big fight before I left for the Olympics. The subject line read "T," signaling the next part of a private game we had going: Pick a letter for the other person, explain the meaning behind your choice, and tell them to rise to the occasion.

The email said:

I pick the letter "T" for you.

We hit a rough patch this year . . .

Stuff came up and stared us both in the face.

It was ugly and it was uncomfortable.

The letter T

Just before we left LA for this trip, you looked at me in your living room, right after we sang the Lana del Rey song together . . . You said, "Kara, the way I've been with you doesn't work for me anymore." You told me how important it was to you that I was a part of your life.

The letter T

How is it that an ugly caterpillar climbs itself onto a tree limb, spins a cocoon, and completely disintegrates itself—only to emerge a butterfly with exquisite colors that can take flight?

Transformation. That's how.

From my heart space to yours . . .

Thank you.

Get it done tonight.

K.

Immediately I wrote back: "T it is."

And in that moment, I meant it.

* * *

We got it done in Wembley Stadium before a booming crowd of 80,203, just a few hundred people shy of being full—the largest audience for women's soccer since the 1999 World Cup final. My support system—parents, siblings, Kara, Are, his mother, Dena, Sarah, and assorted other family and friends—were all there, thanks to Dan Borislow, who paid for their flights and hotels. I was getting chances but couldn't follow through, my headers soaring wide or falling short. But Carli came through twice and we finished 2–0.

When I bowed my head to accept the gold medal, I realized I wasn't ready to face the possibility that it might be the last one I wore. I gave interviews in which I talked about my successful tournament—five goals in six games—and fielded questions about my injuries. They were under control, I insisted, helped by a routine of ice baths, compression stockings, and my boot-shaped night splint, and I would be on the field as long as my body allowed it. "If I can get fully well and feel good, I want to be a part of this team. I think I'm a lifer."

WIFE

I DECIDED SARAH AND I were going to have the best life. Our dreams were lining up, just waiting for us to claim them. As predicted, the Women's Professional Soccer league folded, but a new one sprang up in its place: the National Women's Soccer League, or NWSL, and Sarah and I both played for the Western New York Flash. We lived in Buffalo, an hour from my family, and we both hated it: the cold, the smallness of the town. I reminded her that the season was short—just four months—and then we'd move on. We had faith that something new and exciting would always be waiting for us, as long as we knew where to look.

At age thirty-two, my career had reached its

pinnacle: I'd been named FIFA Women's World Player of the Year, edging out my teammate Alex Morgan and Marta, my perennial rival from the Brazilian team. I scored my 159th goal, breaking Mia Hamm's record for the most goals by any player, male or female. It happened in June 2013, during a game against South Korea; a corner kick found my head and I punched it in, sure and smooth. I was grateful to my teammates, who worked hard to get me the ball, and when reporters inquired about my next goal, I told them this: "I want to give more assists to Alex Morgan so she can break my record." And I meant it; there would be no greater tribute than being surpassed.

For the first time, I had fleeting thoughts about what life might look like after retirement: How would I support myself, and Sarah, and our family? What could an aging athlete with no college degree do? I worried that I wasn't smart enough, that my mind was far inferior to my body and would never accomplish anything on its own. I feared that I didn't know how life worked off the field, and that my purpose would be unsettled and unclear. For the past fifteen years, I'd had a schedule slipped under my door, telling me exactly where I needed to be and what I needed to do; Sarah always joked that I liked the same arrangement even when I was home.

My agent told me not to worry; I'd be fine. I'd be

better than fine. He said, "Believe it or not, Abby, you have more to offer the world than just soccer. People like you. Kids look up to you. Women want to be your friend. Men want to play golf with you. You have valid ideas about politics, about inequality in sports, about advocating for women. You're funny and articulate and can convince anyone of anything. You could sell a ketchup Popsicle to a woman in white gloves. You will know what you're meant to do when that time comes, but for now, just enjoy where you are."

I decided to take that advice.

On a whim, Sarah and I searched online for a home in Portland—friends in the city had been urging us to move—and the perfect one appeared on my screen, as if by magic, as if our wishing made it happen. We sent those friends and a Realtor to check it out: "Amazing views and great bones" was the consensus; with a full renovation, it could look exactly like the picture in our minds. On their recommendation alone, I bought it and appointed myself the general contractor. I wanted to create something out of nothing, a something that would become everything.

I flew out to see the house, the place where I'd have a fresh start. It was perched in the hills outside the city, a perfect balance of bustle and peace. It was made of glossy, warm wood cut in rectangular shapes, the rooms and levels stacked at angles, a structure that reminded me of building blocks. The rear of the second floor featured three French doors leading out to separate balconies. A stone patio ran the length of the property and looked out onto miles of trees. I began making it ours, picking out furniture and lighting and finishes. I visualized the nooks and crannies where our kids would play. We wanted three, maybe. Definitely two, at least. Sarah would get pregnant first, after she retired; I would get pregnant next, after I retired. If things were going well, we'd adopt a third, although they always say the third baby is the divorce baby, and we didn't ever want to let that happen.

My excitement for a baby surged in August, when Kara gave birth to a boy, Lewis. As soon as I heard the news, I rushed to my computer and composed an email:

Kara,

I'm overcome with excitement. I know we've known each other for many years, but tonight really feels so different. You chose to make a baby, and now he's real. Feel that. You made a stand for what you wanted, and now you have this little one who you will love and nurture for all the days of your life. I am more proud of you now than ever. Feel every moment. You made a plan and then saw it through. Do you know how cool that is? I just have the utmost respect for the way you chose life—because it is a choice. And you and I get that.

More than anything, I think you are a lover and a survivor, in all that you do. I had no doubts. Today was a certainty for you. I trust you completely and feel you will be a person in my life I can always turn to. Now I have this to be able to ask you questions about. So cool.

Thank you for being in my life, and giving me the gift of what real love is. It's rare, and a special quality we both have. Just know that today, more than any other, I am sad beyond measure to not be right there by your side. I know you are capable and handled it per-fectly, but to be far and not near is surreal and difficult. What makes it easier is to know that you are strong and will be the best mom in the land. Thank you for the pictures and texts. It meant a lot. Know that I will be doing the same on our blessed day.

We love you beyond imagination. All of you. You, Jenny, Lewis. Can you believe it? You made a human being, Kara. You.

Celebrate that. I think you will look back on this as a time of your life that will always uplift you.

In all sincerity, you are my idol, and I love you.

Now rest,

Abby

While I built our home, supervising every last detail, Sarah planned our wedding. It would be grand but intimate, a low-key ceremony involving our closest family and friends. She decided on Hawaii, and I agreed, because why not? We wanted a destination wedding, a place where people would actually want to go on vacation, a place that would make it worthwhile for my siblings to leave their kids behind for a week. She picked a stunning resort called The Villas at Poipu Kai, on the island of Kauai, envisioning a beach ceremony at sunset: her in a flowing white dress, me in a crisp white suit, wearing matching leis.

We picked a date: October 5. I asked Are to be my best man, and Dena to read a poem. I was thrilled Kara could come, even though baby Lewis would only be two months old. Teammates Sydney Leroux and Alex Morgan planned to be there. Dan Borislow generously offered to pay the bill for the open bar. Our dogs, Tex and Kingston, would be staying behind, but we bought them tuxedos to celebrate anyway. We filed the proper paperwork for a civil union, since same-sex marriage wasn't yet legal in Hawaii.

I was ready. We were ready. I wanted to be as successful at love as I'd been at soccer. It was more important to me than the FIFA award, the Olympic medal, and the World Cup title I hadn't yet won. On the night before the wedding, after the rehearsal dinner, Sarah and I locked ourselves in our suite and wrote our wedding vows.

I was nervous, more nervous than I'd ever been—not because of my wedding, but because my mother would be there to witness it. It was all well and good for her to give her blessing to Sarah in private, but this was public, laid out for the world to see. What would she think when I kissed Sarah after our vows? When we had our first dance? Was she going to stand there wishing I had married Are instead? I confided my fears to Are's mother, Dena, and she assured me that my mother had come a long way—even further than I'd hoped. Once, Dena said, when the three of them were in Orlando watching me play, Are turned to my mother and said, "Your daughter is un-freakin'-believable." And without batting an eye, my mother replied, "I know, she really is."

I laughed. I'd run out of time to be nervous. The procession was going to start soon. I asked Are for the rings, and was horrified by his response: He didn't know he was supposed to handle the rings. My cousin Tracy approached with the rings, saving the day. As Sarah walked down the aisle my heart banged against my ribs. A rainbow appeared in the sky, arching behind her, and I took it as a good omen.

It was immediately followed by a bad one: We realized we'd left our written vows back in the suite, and had to invent new ones on the spot. Still, I'd never heard such a lovely string of words—I could barely believe they were intended for me—and I repeated them on the flight home, hoping they'd always be true.

GAMBLER

ONE MONTH AFTER OUR WEDDING, standing in the kitchen of our Portland home, Sarah made an announcement: She would not play another season for the Western New York Flash. She didn't like Buffalo, and wanted to focus on creating experiences in our new city. Instead, she'd accept an offer to be traded to the local club team, the Portland Thorns.

Looking across the table at her, our dogs running figure eights through our legs, I thought about what to say. Later, after having time to replay the scene, I'd admit some hard truths about myself: I knew I was a bit of a nightmare to live with, with my need for control constantly at odds with my desire to go with the flow. Intense Abby and Chill Abby were in a perpetual showdown, and I wondered if it was me as much as it was upstate New York. But in that moment, without the benefit of looking back, I piled all the blame on her. *I've been here before*, I thought to myself—when Haley admitted her engagement to a man—and the fault line from that betrayal cracked further and deepened.

I wanted to say, "We're newlyweds. We're a family now. If the tables were turned, I'd move to Alaska with you. I just want to be with you, wherever you are. I want you to know you're the most important thing in my life now—more important than soccer."

Instead I said, "Okay, I hear you. I will agree to this decision, but only under one condition: If our relationship starts to suffer, you have to come to New York because I make the most money. That's the most logical step. If you haven't gotten a job and we are doing poorly, then everything needs to stop and we need to reconnect."

We kissed, sealing the deal, and in the spring I moved back to Buffalo, alone.

From the start, I was miserable without her, and I didn't know how to connect to someone who wasn't in the room with me. Texting felt superficial, the phone felt like a job, and Skyping was a poor imitation of the real thing. I got advice from friends who had been in long-term, long-distance relationships, and their responses weren't clear: "Yeah, we don't necessarily talk every day." "We talk every couple of days." "We might text each other to say good morning and good night, but that's mostly it."

These proposed routines were not nearly enough to address my overwhelming need for attention, and I began to get depressed. I thought soccer would be a relief, but it wasn't.

The Algarve Cup is held annually in Portugal. That March, we had our worst showing in history, losing every game in the group stage and finishing in seventh place. I scored only twice during the whole tournament and missed a penalty kick, a shot I've made effortlessly dozens of times. In each game, I noticed that I shut down in the second half—not just physically but mentally, as though a part of me was back with Sarah in Portland, and I realized I would never be 100 percent again.

My failing didn't go unnoticed on soccer chat boards, whose members ripped apart our performance at the Algarve Cup. "Not only did Abby miss a penalty kick (which makes her PK conversion rate about 50% since 2013)," said one analyst, "but her current fitness level let her squander a prime and

easy tap-in for a goal. . . . I recognize her impor-
tance on the field, but when does Abby impede the
future success of the U.S. National Women's Team?"
The next commenter agreed and added, "I still think
she's very much the heart of the team, but I think she
needs to be the heart of the team from the bench. She
spends more time flopping around looking for a call
than she does playing soccer these days."

I had to admit it was true. If only I were half as
talented at flopping around as I once was at playing
soccer.

After the tournament, back in Buffalo, I picked
up my phone to call Sarah. I hated the dial tone, the
ringing, the remote sound of her voice, three thousand miles away.

"You need to come here," I said.

She said no, and explained: She was happy in
Portland. She had a life there. I was so unhappy, and
if she moved to Buffalo, the only thing that was going
to happen was that she'd be unhappy with me, and
that wouldn't be healthy for either of us.

This is not what a relationship should be like, I
thought. *This is not what our relationship* was *like.*
All our interactions seemed tainted by doubt and
suspicion. But I said nothing. I wanted her to think
everything was still okay—I wanted everything to *be*

okay—and if I didn't voice my worries they might stop existing, creep back into some dark corner of my brain.

I fell apart more in June, during a New York Flash game against the last-place Houston Dash, at Sahlen's Stadium in Rochester. In the seventeenth minute, I found the ball and pulled back to take a shot. A Houston defender slithered her leg near mine and tried to block it, and, as I followed through, my foot struck the ball strangely, sending pain up my shin that landed in my knee. *That hurt*, I thought, and felt myself folding to the ground. I was down a minute, and told myself it was going to be okay, even though I knew I'd hurt my knee, and once you've hurt your knee you are never the same. I got up, hobbled around, decided I could play, hobbled around for another minute, and admitted that I couldn't. In the twenty-fourth minute I slumped down on the bench, waiting for the trainers to examine me.

"Check and make sure my ACL is there," I begged, and they moved their fingers around my knee and concluded that it was. I was relieved, and scheduled an MRI the following day for an official diagnosis: a sprain of the lateral collateral ligament, which connects the thighbone to the shinbone, and which was going to take several months to heal.

I decided to view the injury as an opportunity: I was going back to Portland.

I was so excited to be home, to feel the dogs lick my face and smell their terrible breath, to see Sarah in the house I built for us. She was sweet and attentive, ordering me to rest, and despite the fact that she still refused to come to New York, I wanted to believe we'd be okay.

Unfortunately, we weren't. I kept thinking, *I want to be with you more than anything, but I am afraid of being rejected, of once again feeling unloved and unlovable.*

Two more things happened that made that summer the worst of my life. On June 28, a Saturday night, I was driving along Skyline Boulevard, a narrow, twisty road south of downtown Portland. I took a corner too fast and my Range Rover became airborne, spinning, landing on the roof and collapsing into itself, a terrible imitation of my falls on the field. Shards of glass hung in what used to be the windshield. When everything went silent and still, I was almost afraid to move. I wasn't in any pain but was sure I'd broken a limb, or sliced my head open, or crushed my organs till I was bleeding inside. I unbuckled my seat belt, inched my hand toward the door, folded my body, and slid out. The shards fell; I was a second away from being stabbed to death by one. One by one I tested my arms and legs and found all my bones intact. I rubbed my scalp quickly and saw there was no blood on my hands. Miraculously, I was fine, and I looked up and down the road, thankful no one else had been in my path.

Three weeks later, I got a strange message from a teammate about Dan Borislow, my friend and old team owner. She said someone—she didn't recognize the number—texted her claiming that Dan had died of a heart attack, and this person was trying to get in touch with me. I refused to believe it, and then my phone rang, flashing my mother's name. I almost didn't pick up, as if refusing to hear the news would somehow make it untrue.

On the final ring, I answered.

"Is he dead?" I asked, not even saying hello.

"You know?" she said.

By morning, I was in Florida with his family. Dan was fifty-two, and had died after playing a soccer game. In life, he'd played every bit as hard as he'd worked—one of the reasons we connected—and his death was way too sudden. I thought of the last time I'd seen him, at my wedding. The morning after the ceremony, we'd enjoyed a poker game together on the balcony.

I spoke at his service in front of five hundred people. "We love you, Dan," I said, and I turned to his family. "I'm here for you all."

CHAMPION

IN THE SPRING OF 2015 I announced that I wouldn't be playing for the New York Flash in the next season of the National Women's Soccer League. I released a statement, explaining that I needed to prepare mentally and physically for the World Cup tournaments, to be held in Canada in June. I was ready for the criticism—why was I allowed to quit, when my national teammates had to honor their club commitments?—but I wasn't willing to reveal the truth: My time off had nothing to do with the World Cup, and everything to do with my troubled marriage.

Sarah herself was doing well, having retired from soccer and secured a job with Nike, creating an identity outside the sport and making a new group of friends. She had always been dependent on me, and I wasn't used to her having a life so removed from the one we'd started together. I had come home in the hope of closing the distance, but my presence seemed to make it worse. I was the problem no one wanted to mention, the elephant in every room.

She proposed an idea, saying we should delay talking about our issues until after the World Cup. It was my last chance, and she didn't want our problems to change my focus. If I didn't win, I was going to be angry and disappointed and tormented for the rest of my life. She wanted this for me, for us, and she promised to be there for me while I was on the road. I agreed, but I knew soccer would never again have all of my mind or heart.

In the midst of this, my public life was also getting complicated. FIFA had announced that the women, and only the women, would play their World Cup on artificial turf. In the entire eighty-five-year history of the World Cup, which had seen twenty games for men and six for women, the tournament had never been played on anything but natural grass. Resources were not an issue—FIFA is worth billions—and it was clear that their decision was rooted in sexism.

Forget our mounting successes and our increasing popularity. Forget the fact that artificial turf negatively impacts our play, changing the way the ball bounces and rolls. Forget that it also increases the risk of injuries, jostling our joints and taking off a layer of skin each time we slide against it. Forget that taking a diving header on turf is like going headfirst into concrete. It was just one more indication that women's soccer was inferior, that women themselves were inferior, and I decided it was time to speak out.

My teammates were equally outraged. Sydney posted a picture on Instagram of her battered and bloodied shins with the caption "This is why soccer should be played on grass!" Celebrities took notice. Los Angeles Lakers star Kobe Bryant shared Sydney's photo, using the hashtag #ProtectTheAthlete. Tom Hanks followed up with a tweet of his own: "Opinion: Women's World Cup is the best Soccer of the year. Hey FIFA, they deserve real grass. Put in sod." I decided to spearhead a lawsuit against FIFA and the Canadian Soccer Association, charging them with gender discrimination. Forty female international players—from Canada, Brazil, Spain, Japan, and Germany, among others—joined me, and the law firm of Boies, Schiller, & Flexner (the same firm that successfully argued in favor of same-sex marriage) offered to represent us free of charge.

"It's about doing the right thing, and I think this is the right thing to do," I said in an interview. "We have to fight this fight for this World Cup and World Cups in the future. We have to make sure FIFA knows this is not okay. If you were to ask all of them, they know that they would never do this for the men."

Artificial turf was only one item on my growing list of grievances against FIFA. Our coaches are not allowed to hire their preferred staff, a restriction that sets them up to fail. There are differences in the quality of our training: The men's team travels to top facilities around the country, and their expensive equipment—specialty treadmills and weight machines—is shipped along with them. The promotion for our team isn't as good; there was no official Women's World Cup app, and the official FIFA app featured only the men's World Cup. Most infuriating is the pay gap: The men's team makes more money if they lose games than we do if we win. If we win twenty exhibition games—the number we're typically scheduled to play—we would each earn $99,000. For the same feat, members of the men's team would receive $352,000, and would make $100,000 even if they lost every match.

It was difficult for me to identify these inequities when I was in the thick of my career, just thrilled to be getting paid for playing my sport. But with the end looming—along with the realization that I was going to have to find another job—I thought about them every time I put on my uniform and went to work. The lawsuit was all I could do, but I knew the battle had only just begun.

At training camp in Carson City, California, six hundred miles from Sarah, our problems were in my mind, accompanying me onto the field. I was not myself, and everyone knew it, so I decided that the least I could do was admit it out loud. I asked our current coach, Jill Ellis, if we could speak privately.

"Listen," I told her, "I'm serious. However you want to use me, then that's the way I want to be used, because I need to feel like you want my services. I'll do whatever you need. Trust that I will be ready for the World Cup. No matter what, I always am."

As soon as I finished talking, the answer came to me: I'd make sure that my teammates had the confidence that I could no longer summon for myself. Pearcie and I attended meetings with the coaching staff, absorbed all of Jill's concerns and ideas, distilled them into specifics, and conveyed them to the younger players. It was easier for Jill if the captains handled doubts and complaints, if we were the bad cops delivering tough news. Her coaching style was effective—the woman knew how to win games—but she didn't want to criticize her players too harshly for fear she'd distract them. I grew up in a family that did its best to avoid messy emotional conversations, and this was my chance to learn to navigate that terrain.

Every day, after practice, I texted three players an analysis of their performance, tailoring my comments to their personalities—hard truth for some, gentle suggestions for others. I visited others in their rooms, looked them in the eye, and told them I'd been where they were. I'd heard the same criticisms, had the same fears, fretted over things I couldn't control. I reminded them that we were all type-A women, perfectionists who were the very best at what we do, but none of us would ever be champions alone.

I paid special attention to players who usually didn't leave the bench. In past years, there had been one set roster, with a rotation of three or four players who would be called in to substitute. But this year Jill was devising a different strategy, intending to play many people in many games in different positions, and they all needed to be ready. Listen, I told them, what if there's a chance you might start? What if someone suffers an injury, or you perform beyond expectation at practice, or Jill determines it's your time? Don't let anyone diminish you—least of all yourself—and don't be comfortable with your current status. Think about it, and imagine yourself being better than you ever thought you could be.

I hoped my inspirational words concealed my own doubts: My own best days on the field were long behind me, and I thought I might not leave the bench myself.

In May, just before the World Cup, we faced Ireland in an exhibition match. I'd played a full ninety minutes in only four of our last thirty games, and I needed to regain my stamina and sharpness. It was working, and I was feeling at ease on the field, scoring two goals in the first half, the 179th and 180th of my career. In the opening minutes of the second half, I tried for another, lunging my head against the ball and instead connecting with the elbow of the Ireland goalkeeper. My nose took the brunt of it, the hit shifting it out of place and unleashing a river of blood. It streamed through my fingers as I trotted to the sidelines.

"Get me one of those cotton balls, stuff it in my nose, and put me back out there," I told Jill and the training staff. They agreed, and I kept playing, feeling more alive than I had in months.

During the World Cup opener against Australia, I was mentally alert but couldn't translate that feeling to my body. My Achilles tendon throbbed, reminding me of that injury every time I moved my leg. My attempts at headers were awkward, as if I'd forgotten the mechanics of the technique; I was connecting in the wrong spot, miscalculating the distance to the net. We won regardless, 3–1.

In advance of our second game, against Sweden, I had to learn to play the game from the bench. For the first time since 2003, at the World Cup twelve years earlier, I was not in the starting lineup for the women's national team. Throughout the first sixty-seven minutes, I sat and screamed and cheered from the sidelines, and in the sixty-eighth I was called on to substitute for Christen Press. The crowd chanted my name, telling me they still wanted to see me play, that I still belonged here. I didn't score, but neither did anyone else, and the game was a draw, 0–0.

For the next few games, depending on Jill's strategy of rotating the roster, I was in and out, taking my turn on the field and on the bench. I started against Nigeria and, in the forty-fifth minute, blasted the ball in with my foot, scoring the only goal of the game. In the knockout round against Colombia, my foot failed me, hooking a penalty kick wide and to the left. I saw myself miss—the misses were always visible—and I stared at the net in disbelief, my hands covering my mouth. *I'm not my confident self*, I thought, *and someone else needs to score*. Carli and Alex did, thankfully, and we notched another win. I sat on the bench against China, but once again Carli—wearing the captain's armband—came through, breaking a scoreless tie with her head, making it look as easy as I once had.

During the semifinal game against Germany, the top-ranked team in the world, I sat on the bench next to Kelley O'Hara, a twenty-five-year-old wingback playing in her second World Cup. "Stay confident," I told her. "Don't let Jill steal that from you. What if you're called in, and you let her take your confidence for that moment? That moment will be yours. You will shine." And she did, scoring the second and winning goal against Germany.

After the game, she threw her arms around me and said, "That was all you. I would not have survived this tournament, this game especially, if you didn't believe in me."

I pulled away from her so I could look her in the eye.

"No," I said, "that was all *you*. Don't forget you were the one who played. You're the one who put yourself in a position to score."

I'm finished with soccer after this tournament, I thought. *My job here is done.*

Well, almost done. Before the final game, where we'd face Japan, I recorded a seven-minute speech for the team, knowing that would have more of an impact than anything I did on the field.

The Fox Sports studio was darkened, and I sat in the swivel stool, rubbing my hands together and rotating my neck, as if I was warming up to train.

"I might get emotional," I told the crew. "I think I want to do this alone. Are you guys cool with that?"

They were, and they filed out of the studio, leaving the camera running. *The words will come*, I thought. *Just start talking—you've never had trouble doing that.*

"Finally I have a room to myself," I said, and took a deep breath to begin:

"Everybody keeps asking me what this journey has been and what it will mean if we can be on that top podium Sunday night. The days are ticking, and my clock—as it pertains to being a pro soccer player—is coming to an end. But I have a few things I want to get off my mind, and they're all going to be about my teammates.

"I've had the best life. And it's all in total because of the friendships I've made. I've literally grown up on this team, and the good, the bad, and the ugly— my teammates have helped me through it all. And I know that a lot can be said about this World Cup, and how it could be the culmination of my career. And a lot of people have been talking about how this World

Cup has been different for me, and the biggest thing I need to express is my gratitude—to be able to have played for so long, to share the field with extraordinary women."

Tears welled up, and I shook my head in an attempt to stop them.

"I can't believe that I'm even getting emotional on camera," I managed. "It's going to be seen by millions. But the truth is, I wouldn't be here if it weren't for my teammates. I wouldn't have scored the goals that I've scored, or reached the successes that I've had without them. And the only way we win and get to that top podium is if we fight, and we fight, and we fight some more. And I know, no matter what the outcome of the game on Sunday, that we will all have done our best. I know that, in the thirty-five years of life I've had—such a wonderful life—I've experienced so many things I never thought possible. We're talking about women's soccer now. That's something I'm really proud of, whether I'm on the bench or on the field.

"Putting the crest on every single time means something to me. What would it mean to win this World Cup? It would mean everything. But we're one game away. It's not just going to be handed to us, we know that. We know that from the last time around.

We know Japan is going to give us a strong fight. They will not give up. They will not quit. They showed that four years ago; they showed that throughout this entire tournament. We are going to have to play brilliant.

"I want to thank my family. I want to thank Sarah. And my friends who have probably missed me more than anything. People don't get the sacrifices that we make. People don't understand the things that we have to do in order to follow and pursue these dreams that we have. I'm the luckiest person on the planet, and it's not because of any individual award, or even playing on the grandest stage. It's because I've been able to share it. My philosophy in life is that happiness is meant to be shared. And we all have dreams. And if you're out there and you have a dream, and you want something, and you want something so bad . . ."

And here I started crying again, thinking of both soccer and Sarah.

"You've got to risk everything. You've got to risk being completely devastated if you don't achieve it. And when you fall down, you've got to get back up. So that's what this means, that's what this is, that's who we are. This team does not lay down for very long. We have an opportunity to take the world by storm. We have an opportunity to bring back the World Cup, back to the United States. We can do it. I know we can do it. We've just got to go out there for those ninety minutes or those 120 minutes, or whatever that game calls for. We have to bring the fire. I know my teammates are going to do whatever they need to do, because I'm going to do it. Whatever my role is, whatever my job is, whatever I'm asked to do, I'm going to do a little bit extra, because I think that's what's it's going to take.

"It's never easy to say good-bye. You always want to go out on top. You always want there to be that fairy-tale ending. I hope that this is it. Not just for me but for this entire group of women who have showed me the way, who have taught me about myself. Who have made me soul-search and find out more about who I am, and who I want to be. That's what makes this so special. It's not about wins and losses or even championships. It's about learning, it's about growing, it's about being you.

"I'm proud to be a member of this national team. I've been proud since I first got the opportunity to wear this jersey, to represent my country. I hope that people know that nobody's perfect. People make mistakes. But on Sunday, if we make mistakes, I know every single player on the field, every single player on the bench, every fan in the stadium, has our back. That is inspiring. To be a part of it, to be able to look at the stands, and see my family. No matter what happens, I'm going to proud of what we've gotten, and where we've gotten to. I'm a lucky person and . . . I know we can do it. We've just got to believe."

I exhaled, feeling the weight of those words, and said them one more time: "We've just got to believe."

I kept my promise and did my job, did what I was asked to do, which meant leading from the bench. This was the last World Cup I'd ever play in—one of my last games, period—and *man* did I want to play, to churn up the field with my cleats and feel my head kiss the ball. Instead I watched my team deliver an amazing beat-down: one goal at minute three, another at minute five, another at minute thirteen, another at minute fifteen. I almost—*almost*—felt sorry for the Japanese players, wandering around like they were lost on the field. Close to halftime it became more familiar, and they found their way to the goal, slipping one into our net. I remembered my lost high school championship, the last time I wished this hard for a win. For five minutes straight I screamed advice, sending teammates running away from me. Sydney bravely turned to me and gave a stern order:

"Okay, enough." I promised to try. After the break Japan scored again—prompting more screams and running teammates—but we answered in the very next minute, and we made it 5–2.

They were getting desperate, tossing themselves at the ball, and man did I still want to play; I was always the reliable and foolproof closer, and I needed to be on the field as the clock wound down, even if there was nothing to close. I cried as I warmed up, knowing that my team was giving me a gift, and instructed myself to pull it together before I stepped on the field. In the seventy-ninth minute Jill sent me in to replace Tobin Heath. When I reached the line, Carli met me there. She removed the captain's arm-band and wrapped it around my bicep, a gesture I didn't expect but appreciated immensely, a reverse passing of the torch.

The field, even covered in the dreaded Astroturf, had never felt so sweet beneath my feet. Right away I was off, galloping like a Thoroughbred, loving the chase and the capture; an opponent tackled me and earned a yellow card. In the eighty-sixth minute, Pearcie came on. She was forty years old, the last veteran standing from the 99ers, and this was also her last World Cup. Four minutes later the whistle blew and the celebration began; I fell to my knees and raised my face to the sky. When I pulled myself up I saw my teammates, collected in a tight huddle and pulsing like a heart.

But my eyes moved to the left and zeroed in on Sarah, who was wearing a jersey decorated with my name. I lumbered toward her, tentatively at first, and then picked up speed. My arms lifted up and she leaned down, meeting me halfway, draping herself over the railing. I looped my arm around her back; I was worried she was going to fall. She wrapped her hands around my face, fingertips meeting at the back of my neck, and looked me in the eye.

"I did it," I whispered. "*We* did it."

"Kiss me," she commanded.

In the moment, I was not thinking about politics, or the fact that gay marriage had been legalized by the Supreme Court a week earlier. It didn't occur to me that a video of our kiss would go viral, or that I would be asked to say what was running through my mind. Publicly, I said, "In that moment, as a human being, you ask yourself—who's the one person I want to run to, the person who sacrificed with me and dried my tears and wiped my blood and listened to my issues?" Privately, I was thinking, *Even after what we've been through, she's still capable of being there for me. We've set aside all our issues for this, and now it's here, and we won, and it's in the past, and now we can work on finding our way back to each other.*

And so I did as she told me, kissing her like no one was watching at all.

ADVOCATE

DESPITE ALL THE ATTENTION, THE viral video, the headlines declaring that we exemplified "what love looks like," the high from that kiss didn't last. The issues we had before the World Cup only worsened. My marriage became my sole focus, and it began to crumble under the weight of my neediness. Every word was misunderstood, every glance tinged with anger or regret. I wanted what we once had. I chased it, I looked in corners for it. It wasn't anywhere, and I felt lost along with it.

It was a relief when I had to go on the road for the team's victory tour, although initially I had protested the idea. I didn't want the fanfare of a long good-bye, the spotlight on me in each stadium. My teammate Shannon Boxx urged me to reconsider, insisting I owed it to all my teammates and all my fans—that I should think of it as a celebration of not just my career but of all the progress women's soccer had made. It was bigger than just me. I couldn't argue with that. Besides, I thought, maybe the distance would help my marriage this time around. Maybe the act of playing and giving interviews would dislodge my negative thoughts.

It did from time to time. I was secretly thrilled when fans gathered at airports to meet our arriving planes. I joked with reporters that I'd have to revert back to my natural hair color because my current platinum blond made me instantly recognizable. We weren't allowed to sign autographs in hotels, but I always stopped to talk to kids, shaking their hands and telling them to be brave. I talked about gender equality, declaring that I'd keep fighting even though we'd dropped our turf lawsuit. Our lawyers realized that FIFA was going to stall the case, making a decision *after* the World Cup, which made the timing all wrong. I announced that soccer was the next big thing in the United States, and corporations would be smart to get in on the ground floor.

"Get on it, people," I urged. "You guys are going to miss out if you don't. . . . It's an amazing time, not only to be a footballer here in the United States, but to be a female soccer player. We know that bringing home championships just gives us a better platform and another opportunity to start a conversation to get a little bit more pay, and bring that gap closer together."

Every good day was chased by a bad one. I texted with Sarah: "Are we losing something that was once beautiful? Can we ever re-create happiness again?" Neither of us had answers. I became more depressed and restless, especially at night. My roommate on the road, Sydney, once kicked off her covers, pulled out her phone, and retrieved one of her favorite poems. She read it to me softly in the dark:

there will always be
parts of me that only you
can unlock,
that only you can come back to save
and that only you can calm, too soon.
what remains of me,
will always fill
the emptiness in you.
it will always complete all that we have.
the only parts

we have not learned
to say goodbye to.
the only parts where we
can still be free.

I knew it was her way of saying she was worried about me.

On October 27, a Tuesday, the national team visited the White House and met President Barack Obama. The whole event was surreal to me, on multiple levels: Here was a butch lesbian meeting our first black president—a president who decided female athletes were worth celebrating on the most visible stage in the world. "They've inspired millions of girls to dream bigger and, by the way, inspired millions of boys to look at girls differently, which is just as important," Obama said. "This team taught all America's children that playing like a girl means you're a badass."

We'd been warned beforehand not to request selfies, but the president broke that rule. Turning to the crowd, he said, "I'm sure we'd all love to take selfies with them." I decided to go for it. "Mr. President," I said, "how about you taking a selfie with us, then?"

I held out my phone and captured everyone's face but my own; only a streak of my platinum hair appeared along the edge. The best unselfie ever snapped.

As soon as we left the White House, I announced my retirement from soccer, ending my written statement with the words "I can't wait to see what the next chapter of my life brings." I took phone calls from the press, doing my best to redirect the focus back to the team. "It's time for me to walk away," I told *USA Today*. "I know the young studs—the Sydney Lerouxs, the Alex Morgans—they're the ones that will take this game to the next paradigm and that's something I'm excited to watch and see grow. Thinking about my teammates and time spent with them, that's what I'm going to miss most. It's not going to be the sprints, it's not going to be the traveling, it's not going to be—even in some small way—the game. It's going to be the people that I've been literally able to grow up with."

That night, alone in my room at the W Hotel, I crafted a rare prepared speech to give at the next day's luncheon with the National Press Club. I labored over it, organizing my thoughts and fretting over the words; I wanted it to sound like the best version of myself.

"Character is a funny thing," I wrote somewhere in

the middle. "I've found that your character is tested the most when things don't go your way."

Things will be going my way soon, I told myself. *They have to.*

The team's victory tour took a break in November, to be concluded the following month, but I didn't go home. Instead I traveled to San Antonio, Gainesville, New York City, Boston, Washington, DC, Chicago, Milwaukee, Nashville, and Houston. I spoke at fundraisers and attended galas and shot commercials, including one for Gatorade in which I begged everyone to forget me (*but only with regard to soccer*, I thought, *not for good!*). I partnered with Triax Technologies to promote their head impact monitor, and talked about concussion awareness and safety. I recalled how I foolishly stayed on the field after I'd suffered one myself, back in 2013. My teammate, standing a few yards away, kicked a line-drive shot straight to my head, which made me fall like a chopped tree. An opposing player approached and asked if I was all right; I mumbled my answer, my mouth unable to form proper words. Two minutes later, in the last seconds of the game, I attempted to break a 1–1 tie by scoring off a corner kick—using my head.

"I've headed the ball so many times throughout my career, so does it give me pause thinking what my future looks like?" I asked Fox News. "Of course it does, so I want to put athletes in control of their lives so they don't have that kind of pause."

I spoke at a children's soccer fund-raiser, where I saw dozens of sweet, sincere faces in the crowd, and told each and every one of them to make a plan, be confident, and seize every good opportunity that came their way. I felt like I was lying. *You can't even do that yourself*, I thought. At one event, a ten-year-old girl waited her turn in line at my autograph table. I had to look twice; she was wearing my exact hairstyle, buzzed on the sides and longer on the top. She was me twenty-five years ago, had I been brave enough then to defy my mother and cut my ponytail.

"Hey, your hair is so cute," I told her. "Can I take a photo of you for some ideas for my next cut?"

She smiled, squeezing in next to me.

After the click, I brought the girl around to the other side of the table, where no one could hear us, and told her I had a question: "Does anyone think you look like a boy?"

Before she could answer, I spoke again. "It happens to me all the time and it's not something to worry about. See, you and me, we aren't that different at all."

She nodded, her mouth set in a serious line, and I knew she understood.

In Seattle, after an event, I called Haley and asked if I could see her. She lived in that city now with her husband and two children, and she had a job as a social worker at an elementary school. We met at her school and took a walk around the neighborhood, and for once our conversation seemed difficult. Later, she told me she knew something was wrong: I looked unhealthy, pale and thin, and I wasn't the Abby she'd known for years, raw and real. Instead I was "Business Abby," distant and remote, using the voice I reserved for speaking to the press. She asked me how I was feeling about my upcoming retirement, and I reached for the phrases I'd crafted and polished. *It's so exciting, and so many opportunities are falling into my path, and I'm going to be able to make a real difference and have a positive impact on people's lives.* She nodded and said she was so happy for me.

Half the time I was a chatty windup toy, the other half an extinguished fire that would never reignite. My weight went up and down, up and down, my body expanding and erasing itself as fast as it could. I was bursting with confidence and excitement; I was depressed and convinced everything was useless in the end. When I was on the upswing, my ideas created new ideas and I connected with people who could help me make them real.

"I am going to change the world," I wrote to one, "and you will join me. Lots and lots of stuff is happening to create a platform, property, conversation, equal opportunity. . . . Basically create an empire where the sole focus is to make it a normal for men and women to be equals. Not just in sports either. And not just in this country. I want it all. I want it global. The time is now . . . and I'm going to create something to finally get the job done. I am still ironing out a map as to how it will all happen, and I want to form a group of other like-minded badass women to figure out a way to ensure equal opportunity for all human beings happens. Okay . . . I could go on but like I said it would not do it justice. And to be up front, this all has just hit me like a ton of bricks since announcing my retirement. Basically I'm angry I have to find work after my career because I'm a woman. And I'm done with being angry and turning it on its head and just going all in to change it. Now is the time. And I am in a unique position to actually do it.

"Not to be arrogant or overly confident but there is something symbolic about saying you 'will' do something, rather than you 'want' to. And since saying I will change the world, doors that you can't imagine have just swung open and I'm going for it.

"Please let's chat soon!!! I'm fired up. So much work to do, but man isn't this gonna be fun."

It started to dawn on me that I was feeling the way I had as a kid, when I first realized I was good at soccer—not just good, but someone who could be one of the best in the world, doing what I was surely born to do. I could be just as successful at advocacy. "I know I am sounding crazy in every way," I confided to my agent. "But this is how I am processing this. I am so confident right now. Please know I won't lose myself in this, but that in fact I'm finding myself and the voice I want to convey. I am in the brainstorming stage. Some stuff I say and feel is totally crazy, and I get that. I just need to say it and get it out there. Passion is an unpredictable thing. It's not always right or possible. But someone has to have the courage to say what others won't say aloud. . . . We need a plan."

The idea got inside my mind and began to take shape. I pictured an organization whose only goal was pursuing equal pay and working conditions. I would connect with a leader in each industry—media, politics, music, Hollywood—so there was a point person working to make change happen across the board, starting from the grassroots level and eventually lobbying for legislation in Washington. We'd build and grow these platforms, assisting each other's efforts and sharing results. It would be an organization that would grow and flourish with each new generation. We'd reach underserved and underprivileged kids, teaching them leadership skills and inspiring them to imagine a world beyond the one they already knew.

I'd be in charge of the sports sector, working with each individual team to make sure they're on board. I'd point out soccer's awful pay gap: My team split $2 million in prize money after winning the World Cup, while the winning men's German team received $35 million the summer before. I'd argue that FIFA should spend more money promoting women's soccer ($73 million on our World Cup, compared to $2.2 billion for the men) and be more open about its finances; they offer no concrete figures about how much revenue we generate.

Our figures in the United States are equally unsettling. In 2017, the women's team is expected to generate $17 million in revenue compared to $9 million by the men, and yet the men's salaries are still much higher than the women's across the board. For wins, the women's team earns thirty-seven cents to every dollar earned by men. Female players earn between $6,842 and $37,800, while male players earn an average salary higher than $200,000. The growing popularity of women's soccer would help me make my case. Our World Cup final against Japan attracted 750 million viewers worldwide and was the most watched soccer match in US history; our viewership even outdid the 2015 NBA championship featuring Stephen Curry and LeBron James. Even if it was too late to benefit from my own activism, I wanted future generations to be given the respect and compensation they deserve.

I planned to work as hard at striving for equality as I did at perfecting headers. I knew I was stubborn, strong-willed, tenacious. I was fiercely devoted to the concept of fairness. I'd always followed my own path, seeking authenticity even before that became a trendy word, and I could inspire others to do the same. I don't quit. I *won't* quit, no matter what happens.

Except for soccer. I had to quit soccer.

Before I did, though, I had one last month of games for the national team's victory tour. In December, we were scheduled for four matches across the country, beginning in Honolulu and ending on December 16 in New Orleans. We later decided we should cancel our match in Aloha Stadium, since its artificial field looked like it hadn't been replaced in years.

Instead we played Trinidad and Tobago in San Antonio, a 6–0 win, and then beat China in Glendale,

Arizona, my last game. Before the whistle blew, instead of taking charge of the huddle and unleashing my usual words of encouragement, I held back and said nothing. To my delight, two of my teammates stepped forward and ran the huddle, and I knew I was leaving the team—and the game—better than I found it.

After we celebrated, I lay on my bed, trying to freeze my mind, to keep my concerns and fears and hopes quiet for just a few hours, long enough to sleep before they started all over again. My mind ignored my request, and all night I thought of the end of soccer, and the beginning of something else, still wonderfully mysterious and exciting. I thought of Sarah, who planned to come to my last game even though we had no idea what was going on with us. *Retirement is not peaches and cream*, I thought, *and I'll talk about that when the time comes. People don't talk about the hard transitions enough, the hard bits of life. Strength means a lot of things. You've got to be strong from top to bottom, but you also have to raise your hand and say, "I'm feeling weak right now. I need some help." There is true strength in being able to ask for help.*

Without meaning to, I started to cry, tears hitting my pillow, but at least I was strong enough to let them fall. Poor Sydney, trying to sleep across the room, heard me through her earplugs and head-phones. From the corner of my eye I saw her sit up and remove them, then take careful steps to my bed. She lay down and made room for herself, crying right along with me.

CONTROL FREAK

A WOMAN I KNOW SAID something that perfectly captured my thoughts about taking the next step in my life. We were talking about retirement and transitions, the challenges involved in letting go of the only work and life you've ever known. Trapeze artists are so amazing in so many ways, she said, because they are grounded to one rung for a long time, and in order to get to the other rung they have to let go. What makes them so brilliant and beautiful and courageous and strong is that they execute flips in the middle. The middle is their magic. And if you're brave enough to let go of that first rung, she said, you can create your own magic in the middle.

I think about that magic, *my* magic, as I composed an email to my inner circle before the final game:

Hey guys,
First off, I just want to thank all of you for taking the time to come to my last game. Gosh, even as I type that, I feel relief. It's time and I have known for a while.

Anyways, I (with a nudge from a friend) just wanted to write to you guys telling you all the "why" I want all my closest friends and family there with me. And I will totally mess up how I would say it to your faces, so bear with me—I'm a much better talker than writer.

I don't want you guys to feel bad for one moment about the way these few days will go (me being excessive with flights, hotels, etc.). It's gonna be crazy fun, and I wanted to create an environment to in some way SHOW you all how I feel about you and the support you've given me during my time as your friend. You see, I only have—and AM— everything because of the support system that I've been lucky enough to be around.

I know you guys see the "Fun Abby," out at restaurants and going on vacation more often than not, but for the most part of my

life I've been gone, alone, in search of something . . . I think that's why I fell so hard for
every one of you. It's because you can see
me searching for something, and love the
parts of me that don't always equate to this
"pro" athlete, yet you still never judged my
character. I can't tell you how much THIS kind
of personal acceptance you all have given me,
during my time as a soccer player, has meant.

What I *do* know is that your acceptance
HAS defined me!! You all, not the game, have
helped me find myself and a place in this
world. And it's so bizarre to be writing this
and have no idea where my next paycheck
will come from . . . I just want you all there
for me, in my last moments identifying as a
soccer player, to remind me of who I am, and
who I want to be, and that soccer isn't ALL
of who I am. It was a part of the search . . .
Here's the thing . . . what I have found is that I
will always be in search. It's who I am.

Cheers to closing this chapter in my life,
and I can't wait to see what goes on and happens on our next pages together. I wouldn't
want to spend time between these trapeze
bar rungs with any other people. People need
to hold on and feel safe and secure, and I've

had soccer my entire life to secure me and make me confident and make me think I knew who I was . . . These last few years have been a struggle for me in soccer. And so finally, I'm letting go of the trapeze rung and letting some MAGIC happen in the middle.

Before I grab onto the other side, I need some magic (crazy, or danger, or risk, or love, or to let myself become unraveled) and I know, with all you beauties by my side, I will be just fine. I may cry—that's okay, I'm in touch with that part of myself. But what I need you all to know, is that sometimes being in search of something greater doesn't mean it's always out there. Sometimes I may need someone (Sarah) to pull me back home to planet earth.

Quite frankly, I don't know what tomorrow brings, and that freedom for the first time, and truly accepting it, is something new, and something I'm growing fond of minute by minute. My confidence is coming back and reaching that "it" factor I couldn't muster on the field like I used to. I'm honest with myself about that, don't worry. What I do know is I can call on any one of you if I ever need any-thing. And maybe I always overdo it, because

I just want you guys to love me (control freak, and fear of being unlovable) and so I give you anything I think would make you all happy and fulfilled. That is my own stuff I gotta sort through, but this trip is different. It is only a big THANK YOU!! Come, enjoy, and let's see what kind of stuff we can do in the magic. I bet it will be glorious and splendid.

I am the lucky one.

Forever grateful,

Abby

Over the course of fifteen years, from my first appearance in a national game to my last, I developed a pregame ritual. Depending on the quality of my play in any given game, I added and subtracted and modified superstitions, certain that a minor tweak to the formula would set things right again. By my 255th international appearance on December 16, the last game of my career, the ritual looked like this:

Two hours before the whistle blew, I ate a plate of chicken and salad. The chicken serving had to be no larger than the size of my fist, because I wanted to be light and fast. I drank a gallon of water straight from the jug, hydrating myself nearly to the point of nausea, and then tested fate by drinking even more, chugging down a few helpings of Gatorade Pre-Game

Fuel. On the way to the game, I usually called Sarah and played solitaire; on the day of my last game, I did only the latter. I had to win before I reached the stadium, and the number of attempts it took was either a good or bad sign. When I got to the locker room I dropped my bags off, lined up my gear, and removed my jewelry.

First to come off: a family heirloom ring made of diamonds from my grandmother's wedding band, which I wore on my right hand. I slipped it off and laid it in the middle of my locker. Only when it was placed safely in its spot could I begin the task of getting dressed and taped. I pulled on my sliders—the tight underwear that protects your legs from chafing against turf—and then my shorts and a warm-up T-shirt. I was ready to be taped, a complicated, painstaking process that could go terribly wrong, requiring multiple do-overs.

One of my trainers taped my left ankle first, then my right—no reason for the order, but once it worked it became law. I stood up, flexed and pointed each foot, and then headed back to the locker room, where my teammates were all immersed in rituals of their own. Sitting on a bench, I pulled on my socks (first left, then right), my cleats (left, right), and shin guards (left, right). Then it was back to the training room for more taping, where I had to select exactly the right roll of tape. It had to be flat to the touch, with no ridges or wrinkles. Sometimes my trainer would forget and hand me the tape. "No, put it down," I'd say. "I have to pick it up myself." Once I did, I returned to the locker room, handling the roll of tape as though it was a fragile treasure.

It got even weirder.

I plopped down on the bench again and held the roll in the air. In between taping parts of my body and parts of my clothing that needed to stick to my body, I had to rip off a strip, making a clean slate, so that each successive piece of tape had its own specific purpose with no connection to the previous piece. I stuck these "clean slate" strips on my knees, to be dealt with at the end.

But first, carefully, I unfurled a long ribbon of tape and cut it roughly in half, so that the pieces were not quite even. I wound the larger piece around the sock for my left shin guard; the smaller piece was always reserved for the right. If I didn't cut correctly and the pieces looked identical, I had to remove all the tape, fetch a new roll, and restart the entire process from scratch. If I did it correctly, it wound around like a necklace, the two ends connecting perfectly in the back.

I ripped off two clean slate strips, placed one on each knee, and repeated the process, this time taping above each shin guard (left, right). When those were finished, I pressed two more clean slate strips along my knees.

It got weirder still.

The tape also acted as a substitute for my rings, both my grandmother's and my wedding band, since we were not allowed to wear jewelry when we played. By the end of my career, I could easily yank a piece of tape so that I ended up with just the right amount, a width that accurately reflected my level of neediness: a thin strip if I was feeling confident, a thicker one if I was not. I wrapped one piece around my right ring finger and another on my left, a sign to my family and wife that they were with me on the field. On this night, for the first time, I left my left finger bare; Sarah and I were not even in a place where I wanted her represented by a strip of tape. She'd be at the game, sitting in box seats, and I knew she'd notice its absence.

I couldn't think about her then; I needed to add two more clean slate strips to my knees, so that I now had six total, three on each side. It was time to discard them, which involved an entirely separate ritual. One by one, I ripped off the pieces on the left knee, and folded them into themselves so that the corners precisely aligned, creating a triangular wad. I found the trash and released each wad with a flick of the wrist, spinning them like helicopters into the can. If the wads didn't spin properly, or if I missed, I had to attempt all three again.

But by then, the damage was done, and I was convinced it was not my day. Regardless, the entire process then had to be repeated on the right side.

It wasn't over yet.

In games past, when Rachel Buehler was still on the team, her pregame routine had been a vital part of my own. She sat by her locker and retrieved pictures of people and things she loved. I looked not at her photos but at her face, watching her reactions. Now, without Rachel here, I took a peek at Alex Morgan, who, before every game, curled herself into a ball at the bottom of her locker, head clamped between her knees, finding quiet amid the chaos.

When we were ready for warm-ups, I had to be the first one out of the locker room; everyone was aware of and complied with this quirk. Of course, I had to lead with my left foot, and my left foot had to touch the field first. Then I backed away and stepped directly on the line, left then right. Now my crazy was sufficiently quieted, and I could begin to move, jogging a few laps before I stretched each leg, left and right.

Then the crazy resurfaced.

I found a ball and juggled it twenty-five times

underneath my knees. On the last one, I popped it up, trying to trap it on its way down. If I succeeded, I knew I was going to have a good game (a successful trap might even prevent the damage done by a poorly aimed wad of tape). I made it my job to grab the practice jerseys—or "pinnies"—for the game, always handing the first one to Pearcie. During drills, I had to score, kicking the ball through the gates. If I missed or hit a cone, the successful juggling no longer mattered, and I was doomed.

Sometimes it helped, especially toward the end, to lay blame anywhere but on myself.

We took off our pinnies, threw them down, and moved on to our official shooting practice. "Let it ride," I said to whoever was covering the goal, and they knew not to block the shot. Practice was the only time I could witness the ball hit the net, and I tried to carry that image with me for when it would actually count.

I had to be the second one back in the locker room; our goalkeeper, Hope, was always the first. She engaged in her own pregame ritual, changing her whole outfit, down to her socks.

"Here we go, Hope!" I said.

"Here we go, Abs!" came the immediate reply.

For as long as I could remember, it had been our

standard call-and-response, as automatic as amen after a prayer.

We were almost there.

Everyone lined up to go to the bathroom, and I had to use the middle stall. Pearcie summoned us over for our pregame pep talk, reminding us of strategy, of tricks our opponents might attempt. Everyone trickled out onto the field and I was the last in line. Our coaches were waiting for us, lined up in a row with their hands raised, prepared to give high fives. When I reached them I pulled my hand back and snapped it forward with every ounce of strength, intent on making these high fives the most solidly executed and painful in high-five history. I approached the field, making sure that once again the left foot tapped the grass first.

When the national anthem came on, I lowered my head, closed my eyes, and pictured myself scoring a header goal. After the words "home of the brave" faded, I hopped lightly, three times. Back at our bench, someone handed me water. I squirted two shots into my mouth, spit it out, and then sprayed water all over my hair and shook my head like a freshly bathed dog. With my face still wet, I slapped my cheeks three times as hard as I possibly could; the sound and the sting were the last signals to my body, assurance that it was ready.

At long last, there was the huddle on the field—my yelling, my stammering, my leading the "Oosa" chant—and then I found my position, jumping as high as I possibly could and pretending to make a header, my eyes connecting with the net while they still could.

It was over, and it was just beginning.

My coach and my teammates insisted on starting me, even though I was ill prepared and unfit, for once underweight instead of over. The crowd, all 32,950 of them, transformed my name into a song—*AB-BY WAM-BACH (clap clap, clap clap clap)! AB-BY WAM-BACH (clap clap, clap clap clap)*—and the beat lingered in my ears long after they stopped. People waved enormous cardboard cutouts of an earlier version of my face, pinker and plumper. I hung over the railing, a red, white, and blue banner made to resemble Obama's "Hope" poster. Earlier that day the president had tweeted about my last game: "Congrats on a great career, Abby Wambach. For the goals you've scored & the kids you've inspired, you're the GOAT!"

The whistle blew, and I did not feel like the GOAT (meaning "greatest of all time"). In fact, before the game, I hadn't even known what that meant; I thought the numerous Twitter mentions were insults and accusations that I had finally been exposed, and my agent had to reassure me that wasn't the case. Now my teammates took every chance to pass me the ball, but it seemed like a live thing, moving on its own, rolling out of reach every time I got close. I was sad, and by the middle of the first half, I started screaming: "We need a goal! Don't worry about trying to get *me* a goal—*we* need a goal!" They kept passing the ball to me anyway, and my best shot, from twelve yards out, rolled weakly toward China's net. At halftime, in the locker room, my teammates took turns apologizing to me. There was nothing to be sorry about, I told them. Today was not about getting a result. It was about celebrating our team and the time I'd spent with them.

In the seventy-second minute, Jill called me off, and the sound of applause followed me to the bench. *Symbolic*, I thought. *I had seventy minutes and I can't score. It really is time for me to step away.* No one else scored, either—they had spent all their time passing the ball to me—and we lost, 1–0, our first defeat on American soil in 104 games.

Privately, I was devastated beyond measure. I did not want to lose; I had never in my life been comfortable with losing. I wanted it to end, but not like that. I didn't want that stumbling, slow-motion performance to be the last recorded footage of my career. I was also worried about my own postgame celebrations.

My family was unaware of my marriage troubles, and I could only imagine the fake-cheery conversations Sarah had been having with them, the imaginary narrative she was stitching together. Would she tell them I asked her to skip the after-party? That I was too afraid of us fighting and making a scene and ruining the whole night? At the same time, I was amazed that she had come at all, once again ignoring her own hurt and pain just to support me. *With soccer ending*, I thought, *I might finally be able to show up for her. The real me, not the me I am right now.*

Standing in the center of the field, thousands of pieces of cardboard with my face on them waving back at me, I took the microphone and addressed the crowd. "I'm going to make this short," I said. "I love you guys. I love this team. I love my country. And it has been my pleasure and honor to represent all of you for as long as I've been able to."

Someone high up in the stands screamed, "Thanks, Abby!" the words so loud and clear it was as if he whispered them face-to-face.

"My family, my friends, you guys in the suites"—I thought of Sarah but didn't say her name—"I wish I was there right now. But I think symbolically, the way this game went, means that this team, and for me it means I can walk away. The future is so bright. These women are going to kill it. I know it. And before I get all emotional, I just want to genuinely express how much I have given myself to this team, and how important"—I had to pause to stop myself from crying—"and how important it is to give all of yourself to whatever you want to do in your life as a passion."

I turned toward my team. "I love you guys so much," I said.

I dropped the mic on the field with a muted thud.

Wambach, *out*.

WORK ADDICT

I STOPPED SLEEPING. I COULD stay up until six in the morning and be at breakfast by eight. I had much to do, to see, to think about, to plan. Hillary Clinton's people asked me to campaign for her after the holidays. The president of Equinox, Sarah Robb O'Hagan, congratulated me on my "amazing year" and told me she couldn't wait to witness the next phase of my life. To that end, could she introduce me to Wharton professor Adam Grant? He was planning the next People Analytics Conference and thought I'd make an interesting addition to the lineup. I spoke with Tim Cook, who agreed that treating people equally and fairly is ultimately good for business. At the Facebook offices in San Francisco, I met for hours with Sheryl

Sandberg in a glass-walled conference room, situated like a giant fishbowl in a hallway maze. "Stick to your guns," she told me. "Focus on the feminist aspects of inequality, and the rest will work itself out."

On another visit to Facebook, I tried the not-yet-released Oculus Rift, a virtual reality device that immerses you in a futuristic, three-dimensional world. The Facebook employee slipped the headset over my ears and asked, "Are you creative?" I told him no, not at all, but as I worked the controller and wandered through this alternate universe, I reconsidered my response. Isn't rebellion a form of creativity? My lifelong search to find alternative routes to be better and faster, to excel at the highest level with minimal effort? Even *this*—my all-consuming obsession with changing the world—involved a creative suspension of disbelief: If I directed my energy outward, on forces and factors far away, I wouldn't have time to examine the wreckage all around me. I could control what I envision for others, but my own life plan had been changed forever.

I briefly went home—not to Portland but to Rochester, where the town threw me a retirement party and I wept multiple times onstage. Most of the attendees had known me since childhood—teachers and coaches and the local paper's sports journalist—and a part of me longed to go back in time, to wake up on a day when my biggest problem was breaking my curfew. Mercy's field had been renamed the "Abby Wambach '98 Field." Current soccer players for Mercy talked about why they admired me. "She holds herself in a way where she's not cocky, but she's very determined and passionate," said one team captain. "She inspires a lot of young women to want to be better," said the other. "It's just amazing."

My sister Laura told favorite family stories: One Christmas I insisted that everyone do a random act of kindness; mine was to leave money in a copy of *The Giving Tree* at the local Barnes & Noble. I used to lick each French fry so none of my siblings would want to eat them, and I'd have the whole plate to myself. Last summer I held fishing contests for my nieces and nephews at our house in the Thousand Islands, promising $600 wireless Beats by Dre speakers as the prize. "We don't accept ties," I warned them. "There's only one champion. Get out there and fish—we need a winner." Afterward I apologized to them for being so tough, and explained that I was trying to teach a valuable lesson: Life makes people work for what they want.

My nephew Ben thanked me for inspiring him to be a better teammate and person. He would never forget a question I once asked him: "Who do you want to be and how do you want to get there?" My mother imagined all the exciting things I was going to do with the talents the good Lord had given me. The local sports reporter, who had covered my career since high school, called me a role model and a "guiding light" and said he couldn't deliver a bigger compliment than this: If his two-year-old daughter grew up to be half the woman I was, he'd be a lucky, lucky father.

I took the stage to deafening applause. "If you dream anything, if you want something, just go after it," I said. "You might surprise yourself."

From Rochester I flew to New York City for business meetings. My agent traveled with me, making sure I kept to my schedule, compiling notes and ideas for my "equality manifesto." Before we parted ways he took me aside.

"Are you okay?" he asked. "You need to take care of yourself. You look tired and unhealthy." I agreed, and I spent the rest of that trip lying in bed, trying to fall asleep. I couldn't stop yawning, but I still couldn't sleep. I was working too hard, stretching myself too thin, and I hated the world. I hated myself. Unbeknownst to me, a few concerned friends had begun to hatch a plan; they called it "Operation Get Abby Back."

On December 21, I flew back to Portland, exhausted.

* * *

When I got home, Sarah and I had the worst fight of our marriage. I was gripped by the need to remove myself from the situation. I threw clothes and toiletries into a suitcase, started up my car, and headed south to Los Angeles. I thought of the trip I took eleven years ago, back in 2004, when I drove thirty-two hours straight from Florida to Phoenix to see Haley, to hear her admit in person that she was dating someone else. On this trip, I didn't eat, I didn't sleep, I stopped only to check my emails and block Sarah's phone number and email. *I need to go in search of happiness*, I thought. *There are too many highs and lows, too much back-and-forth between incredibly awesome stuff and moments where I have no idea what I'm doing or who I am. Why is it that when one part of my life ends, every part of my life ends?* When I arrived in Los Angeles, it was twenty hours later, and Kara opened her door to let me in.

I stayed with Kara for a week, until I felt calm and settled. *I can do this*, I told myself. *I can stop running away from my relationship and running too hard into work. I will stop feeling like a failure, like I'm less than, and be excited about the future. All my life I've done only exactly what I wanted, and I can do this.*

The next day, I was back at work, exhausting myself again.

I flew east to join Hillary's campaign the first

week of January. Lena Dunham was there, too, and before the event she sent me a text: "Do you have your speech all planned out?" I panicked; I had no speech, not even a loose outline prepared, and so I texted my agent: "What speech? You didn't tell me I needed a speech, like a proper speech." His response was immediate and reassuring: "No, it's not a proper speech. It's what you do—you just do your thing. You just go. You're the best at it."

When we arrived in Portsmouth, New Hampshire, I spoke first. I said that being able to envision a female in the Oval Office is exactly what I'd been working toward my whole life. I'd just retired from playing professional soccer, something that wasn't even possible fifteen years ago, and now here we were, possibly having a woman as president. Scratch that—it wasn't *if* Hillary got into office, but *when*.

I waited for the cheers and applause to stop.

I continued. I didn't support Hillary just because she's a woman. I wholeheartedly believed that our country, by and large, is socially conscious, and if you examined her plans and ideas and goals, it made sense to vote for her. And I believed that everyone was inherently worthy of opportunity; everyone deserved a chance. Even if you were a minority, even if you were a woman, even if you were different colors, different races, different orientations. And to me, she represented someone who gave all minorities in our country a positive mind-set: If she could do it, I could, too.

More cheers and applause, and then I brought it home:

"The symbolism of a female president is incredibly exciting to me. Imagine a fifteen-year-old girl looking up to a woman president and walking a little taller, feeling a bit more confident, beginning to imagine that *she*, too, could achieve that office. And then imagine a fifteen-year-old boy, looking at his classmate and thinking she could be president one day—a slight shift in gender norms that could have a long-term ripple effect, eventually changing the world and the way we all operate in it. It's very exciting, and I'm looking forward to watching Hillary Clinton make it happen."

Lena Dunham approached me afterward and said, "I think you're the most charismatic person I've listened to speak, ever."

"Come on," I argued, rolling my eyes.

"No," she insisted. "You're really good at what you do."

I thought of all the people she must know—writers and actors and artists who get paid to craft and deliver words. I was honored by the compliment, and impressed that she went out of her way to tell me.

"Thank you," I said, simply, and reminded myself that I was proving myself in a place that had nothing to do with soccer, that my value did not end when I stepped off the field. *I can do this*, I thought. *I am doing this.*

While I built my new platform, researching equality issues and meeting people, my marriage continued to have troubles. Sarah was angry at me for leaving Portland so suddenly, for choosing to run away rather than face our problems head-on. When we sent texts, our exchanges were brief and suggested that the best thing to do might be to end our relationship rather than repair it. I had no idea what I needed or even what I wanted, and I shared my misery and confusion with Kara.

"It's so sad," I texted. "It's hard to quit her and the life that we built. But it became a fantasy and not reality. That is what I do know now. It's been so hard to keep silent from her. Like the hardest thing I've ever done. It makes me mad, tho. Loving someone so much that you actually have to let them go."

"Yep, the worst," Kara agreed.

"And I won't ever stop loving her." I added, "I want to get fit again. So I am gonna focus on that. ☺."

But my mind inevitably returned to the negative, bringing up the thoughts I'd worked so hard to bury.

187

Within a half hour I was texting Kara again: "I have known for my whole life I wanted to be a mother. And I'm so mad that I can't do that right now. I've waited for years to be done playing for that experience. And I can't blame Sarah. It's my fault, too."

Kara encouraged me to go away, carve out some time to reflect and relax, and to keep relying on my friends. "If you really want to find yourself," she wrote, "you need to keep close to everyone who loves you."

"A retreat could be the answer," I said. "I have to stop worrying about the plan I used to have about what my retirement was gonna look like."

"Surround yourself with people that you can grow with," she urged. "People who challenge you and don't give you a hall pass on being your best self."

"I have to accept what I hear . . . we are our environment. And Sarah challenged me to be a better person and not continue with my patterns. I didn't want to change for her. That's why I left. I want to change for me. I know I married her because she would never let me get too lost. But here I am, needing to do it alone . . . I am lost. And it's ok. I accept that this is my life."

I thought about the Rochester retirement party, that idolized version of myself that everyone believed was the real me. There was so much I wanted to do, and yet so much I wanted to undo, and I didn't know how to resolve the two.

"I have to hold my younger self and love on her," I said.

Kara knew exactly what I meant. "Hold her in your arms and tell her. Ask for her forgiveness. She's your pure self. The un-jaded one."

"I know," I wrote, and couldn't help but smile thinking about her; in my mind, my childhood self was an entirely different person. "She was so cute and always needing a shower. Haha. The one who has never had her heart broken. I have to learn how to be alone. And be ok with it."

"You know how you always say you're unlovable?" she asked.

"I know logically I'm lovable," I replied, and thought of how that worry plagued me as a kid—knowing I was different, and believing that difference was a burden. "But deep down I have a scar from long ago."

"Forgiveness is an act of self-love," she said. "You've suffered enough. You owe it to yourself, dude."

I had to muster the will to type my next words: "My self-loathing has been killing me."

"You're coming down now," she pointed out. "You're slowing down and processing it . . . I understand self-loathing. However, don't stay too long with that. There's no power there. There never will be."

"I want peace," I said, exhausted from the exchange. "Deep peace nothing can shake."

Toward the end of January, I took Kara's advice and rented a house in Manhattan Beach for three weeks, intending to slow down and center myself, to start off the new year in a positive frame of mind. This year, 2016, is the year of the monkey, and I was born in 1980, another year of the monkey, which I took as a good omen. I planned to spend part of the time by myself and invited a group of friends, including Sydney, to join me for the rest. I was excited for my friends to see me in a state where I wasn't crazy and running around. Where I wasn't working myself to death. I hired our World Cup chef to come cook healthy meals. Those three weeks would cost more than a year's worth of mortgage payments on my house in Portland, but it was worth every cent.

When Suzi the chef arrived, she went shopping for organic fruits and vegetables and gathered us all in the kitchen while she did her magic. I took pictures of her beautiful meals and posted them on Instagram, ignoring the commenters who asked me why Sarah wasn't there with me. I surfed and posted pictures of myself in my wetsuit, and ignored more questions about Sarah. I thought about who I was with her versus who I was by myself: *Am I afraid of being alone because I love Sarah, or because I'm just afraid of being alone? Was she my rock, or was I my rock, and I gave her more power than she should have had?* Every night I sat on the balcony and watched the sunset, taking comfort in knowing that the same view would greet me again tomorrow.

In February I visited my parents at their condo in Florida, intending to help my mother recover from knee surgery. Sarah and I were at least texting again, trying to figure out what went wrong. We acknowledged we really had something good, and we messed it up. Either we had to accept what happened and move forward together, or we had to accept what happened and move apart. At that moment, we were apart more than not, taking turns staying in the Portland house, leaving before the other one arrived.

I asked myself hard questions: *Can I accept responsibility for the things that happened, the things I caused? Can I accept responsibility for the hurt I've caused? That's why people get divorced—because they can't deal with the sad feelings they created. And until you can get right and accept the fact that you've shattered somebody, that you've broken their heart in more ways than one, there's no way that you're ever going to be able to survive.*

I started a new diet and eliminated certain foods: coffee, cheese, meats, refined sugars and flours, white bread, and, of course, all junk food. *It's only thirty days*, I told myself. *I'm an extremist; I can do anything for thirty days.* I was addicted to this diet while I was on it, 100 percent committed, and I figured—while I was at it—that I should work on balancing my obsessive personality.

I continued unleashing my thoughts: *I need to work on the balance of letting go a bit and letting other people be themselves. I did not let Sarah be herself.*

I kept waiting for the thoughts to tire themselves out, to sit down and take a rest. But still they came, rattling through my mind like an express train.

I spent two hours signing soccer balls, posters, and T-shirts. I went golfing with my dad. I took my mom to her physical therapy appointments and recalled a conversation we had shortly after my last game; she could read the misery in every line on my face, every movement of my body. "Abby," she'd said, "I am your mom and it's okay not to be okay."

"Mom," I protested, "it's *not* okay for me not to be okay. And I don't feel comfortable talking about not being okay with many people." And then I said something as difficult for me to admit as it was for her to hear: "I especially don't feel comfortable talking about it with you, because I do still feel a sense of abandonment from my childhood, a fear that I was and am unlovable and unloved."

Later, I realized that voicing those thoughts was a breakthrough in our relationship, one I'd been wanting and working toward for years. *I do feel comfortable talking about it with her*, I thought, *because I actually had that conversation. I let her see me at my worst, and let her hear me admit it. And I came to Florida to help her heal, but she is also helping me.*

I checked my phone for texts from Sarah, who was off snowboarding for the week with friends, and I feared she and I would never go away together again. I feared we'd never even live together again.

On the weekend of March 11, I flew out to Kansas City to see Sydney and her husband. She was pregnant with their first baby and had planned a gender reveal party, and I wanted to be there, for both her and myself. I wanted the contact high of someone else's joy, and the possibility of taking some of that feeling home.

I stayed for four days so Sydney and I could have some time alone. The reminder that I might not have a child with Sarah took over every thought, and I just wasn't myself. I was distant and confused. Sydney and I talked for hours, just like the old days, but she was looking at me strangely, as if I was speaking some language only I could understand. I brushed it off and launched into a funny story, but that strange look stayed on her face.

"You've already told me," she said.

I brushed it off and launched into another funny story.

"You've already told me," she said.

I brushed it off and launched into another story. From her expression I could tell what she was thinking: She'd heard this one, too. Instead of saying anything, she took pity on me and let me keep talking.

When my plane landed in Portland, I decided to explain why I'd been so strange.

"I'm having a breakdown," I texted Sydney, "because I know what I need to do on this trip. Give me strength. Please, I'm begging you. I'm in a taxi to my house. And it will be empty without Sarah the whole time, but I'm just so confronted by it all right now."

"Take deep breaths," she responded, "and just believe that everything will be okay because it will be and it always is. You always told me that 'In the end it'll be okay.' You said that to me a million times and now you have to believe it."

"Okay, I will breathe," I wrote, inhaling as I typed.

"I want my life back. I have to love myself again, which I have started to really do. No joke. Just being here makes me feel like a child, and brings up all these emotions that make me crash. I want you to know I need to lean on you and for you to tell me the hard things I need to hear. Don't tell me what will make me feel better in the moment, but what will make me a better person. I know you have always done that. Need it more now than ever."

I was relieved to see the message bubble; she was still there.

"I want you to be happy again," she said. "And you're not happy, you're just numb. I can't imagine how hard this is but you are NOT alone. If you need me to fly to Portland right now or to follow you around because you're scared of what it feels like to be alone in your own thoughts, I am right there with you. Pregnant or not, I am there."

"Thanks, Syd," I typed. "In tears reading this. But I am strong and haven't been for so long. I will get stronger. That I know. I have been getting stronger. It's just that being here makes it hard again, you know? I love you and thank you for loving me for just being me and my crazy self."

The taxi pulled up to my beautiful, custom home, quiet and empty. I sat at my kitchen table and couldn't bring myself to move. I pulled out my phone and texted Syd again: "I have been choosing to be sad. I know it. Hoping a miracle would happen . . . I know what needs to happen to truly move on. And running wasn't the answer."

Thankfully she was still there: "It never is," she said. "Seriously, the only thing that's going to help is time."

"I'm impatient. And I hate that I have this fancy home. I built this for my future, and now it's empty with no love." I thought about the other future I'd been building—the advocacy platform, the old girls' club—and shared a fear I hadn't been able to admit, even to myself: "I'm afraid my life won't lend me to any truly loving relationships. I can make myself as busy as I want, and I will because it's all I know . . . My schedule, Syd. And what I do and will do. No one would want that."

"You WILL!" she insisted. "Because you deserve it. Someone who loves you for exactly who you are and not who they want you to be."

"How do I sell this house then? And how do I move on? I want to be happy again."

She offered practical advice: "You sell the house. You move to wherever you want, and you pick yourself up off the ground as you've done many times before, and you put one foot in front of the other. That is the only way. And you put your heart and soul into being a better person for YOURSELF and no one else."

"Yeah, that sounds nice," I agreed. "I want to love me again. Be proud of myself again."

When I put down the phone, I was full of confidence. *You can do this.*

FAILURE

ON THE LAST DAY OF March, Sarah and I had another blowout fight—one that convinced me, finally, that we were really and truly over. We stood in our kitchen, in the beautiful, loveless house, and hurled our words, each one sharper than the last. We'd created a mess that extended beyond the two of us, with all our friends having to choose sides and split their time. I was being pushed out of my city, exiled from my own life, and I was both discouraged and furious.

"This happened," I said. "This is happening. The least you can do is go and apologize to all of our friends for putting them in such an uncomfortable position." With each breath I regained an inch of control. "Now I'm going to take care of myself," I declared. "I'm drawing up divorce papers. I'll move out, you'll move out, I'll sell my car, you'll sell the other car, we'll get new stuff, get new everything, and start over."

I secluded myself on the opposite side of our house, as far away from her as I could be without leaving. I was still so upset at the idea of selling but couldn't imagine staying there, trapped in four thousand square feet of ruined paradise, surrounded by the ghosts of dead dreams.

I was furious when I fell asleep.

The following morning, I woke up with a sense of purpose. There were practical tasks I had to accomplish to move forward. I packed up my most valuable possessions, stashing them all in my car. I searched online for a temporary apartment to rent, any place that was clean and would accept me quickly, and then got a hotel room downtown. I wandered the hallways, feeling like I was on the road in my own city, the only member of my own visiting team. I called Haley, silently urging her to pick up.

"Hey, Hal," I said, breezy and upbeat.

"Oh. Hey," she said, and her words sounded odd, short with just a bit of rage.

Cheerfully, I asked how she'd been and what she'd been up to since I saw her in Seattle, back in the fall.

Silence, and then she asked, "Don't you remember our last phone call?"

I thought, willing the memory to come. Nothing.

"No," I admitted. "Why?"

And she proceeded to tell me. In December, just before my last game, I called her. I was upset, and confided that my marriage was in trouble, and I wanted nothing more than for her—Haley—to join me in New Orleans, to be by my side during my last game, and possibly beyond. She thought it was inappropriate and out of character; we'd always respected each other's marriages and boundaries. After that, she didn't want to talk any further; in fact, she wasn't sure if she'd ever want to talk to me again.

I apologized, and wished I could take so much back—words both remembered and forgotten.

I wanted to go home, just for now.

When I finally made my way back to my house it was nearly dawn, a pink fingernail of sun inching up the sky. Sarah was inside in her bathrobe, waiting for me. The way she leaned against the door of our kitchen—arms crossed, face expectant—reminded me of Jake at the end of the movie *Sixteen Candles*, hoping it wasn't too late to get the girl.

Suddenly, instead of crying, I started laughing instead.

I will get better, I thought. *And I have no choice but to go forward.*

HUMAN

I'VE MADE SO MANY DECISIONS that have taken me away from myself, that have made it impossible to know who I am, and I'm ready to chart the path back. Intense Abby assures me I can succeed, and Chill Abby reminds me that a happy life still includes moments of pain.

Lately, I've been doing a lot of speaking engagements. Recently I attended the People Analytics Conference at Wharton business school, and when I started speaking, I was grateful to be onstage with a clear mind, a sharper picture of who I am and what I can contribute. I worried it wasn't much—I felt out of my league among these brilliant academics—but afterward Adam Grant praised me. He asked if I would return to teach a class on creative management, emphasizing realness and the power of confronting your past. I told him I'd be thrilled.

I especially love speaking at colleges; the audiences are full of people who have yet to make bad decisions, people who can still learn from my own. At each school—the University of Kentucky, Penn State, and Georgetown—the auditoriums are filled with students willing to hear what I have to say. Each time, my mind rewinds to one of my first post-retirement appearances: the kids' community soccer league, where the negative commentary scrolled through my brain and I felt like a liar. Every time, I have no speech prepared, and when the light drops down on my head, following me across the stage, I do what I've always done and just start talking, hoping the words land right.

I talk about my family and being raised on competition, the bruises that covered my body after long days playing with my brothers. I talk about my first devastating failure, losing the state high school championship, and how it propelled me to try harder and never give up. I talk about how it paid off the following year, during my rookie season at Florida, when—clever little brat that I was—I took over my team's huddle and announced that we were *not* losing. I talk about breaking my leg before the 2008

Olympics: the difficulty in staying home, the humility in realizing that my team didn't need me to win. I talk about my last World Cup, and the hard, cold realization of knowing my time was almost up, that the one defining skill of my life has faded and dulled. I talk about summoning the will to lead from the bench, telling younger players to seize their chances, that the future is theirs to define.

Then I flip the conversation, addressing the students directly. You should defy labels, I tell them, whether created by others or yourselves. You should become comfortable with conflict and disagreement; you should not be afraid to speak your mind. You're going to bring about real change; the world is out there, waiting to hear your voices and mark your steps. It's not your failures that define you but how you react to them and use them to change. You should all ask yourselves three questions: Where do I want to go, how do I want to get there, and why?

Almost every time, I believe my own words, and I know I am on my way to finding the answers.

EPILOGUE

IT'S EARLY, THE SUN STILL too low to cast shadows, and I'm running along the streets of Paris, letting myself get lost, a routine I established as soon as I arrived. Soccer has taken me all over the world but never allowed me to see it beyond the hotel rooms and training facilities and fields. So though I've visited Paris many times, this ancient city is new to me. It suits me, this atmosphere of discovery, of not knowing where every twisty path might lead.

I'm here for three weeks, covering the Euros—Europe's championship tournament for men's soccer—for my new job with ESPN. The Eiffel Tower looms to my right. My data watch beeps alerts about my heart rate and speed, a sound that will always be familiar. I cross the bridge to the south side of the Seine and pick up speed, weaving around pedestrians, catching snatches of mysterious conversation. I pass floating gardens, the Musée d'Orsay, the Louvre. At the Pont des Arts, the bridge famously weighted with thousands of love locks, I think of Sarah, back in Portland, in the house I still don't call home.

All of our anger and blame, smoldering for years, have finally put themselves out. When the smoke cleared, I admitted all of my faults—both what I'd done and what I failed to do. I never gave her enough credit for encouraging me to confront my issues. I never gave myself fully to her, because I'd long ago given myself to soccer. I tried to split my time and devotion between the two and ended up failing at both. Our future together is still uncertain, but now the good memories have asserted themselves, reminding us why we once worked so well, and of the gifts we've given each other. I've spent my whole life running—from pain, from fear, from myself— and without her I never would have stopped.

On my fourth day here, I arrived at the studio to provide my first commentary on a game, Slovakia versus Wales. I am used to performing for an audience but my body has always done the work; even as I sunk into my chair, I worried my mind might not be up to the task. The men's game is foreign territory, with its own history and nuances and rules, and it will take time to know it as well as I know my own game. So I approached the job as I approach every-thing: from the gut. *I'm going to stick to what I know and what I'm good at*, I told myself. *And what I'm good at is faking it.*

Moments after the camera began rolling, I realized my mistake. *Wow*, I thought. *That was epically hor-rible.* Another realization: I don't know if I'll ever be skilled at this, no matter how hard I try, and that's okay. I'm not always going to be good, I'm not always going to win, and I'm no longer afraid of failure.

I keep running. I pass the gargoyles of Notre Dame, pensive and menacing and hideous. I veer off into a labyrinth of alleys, long stretches of cobblestones that seem to narrow with each step, as if leading to the point of a cone. Storefronts blur past: *fromage*, *boulangeries*, patisseries, the last a reminder that I'm still forgoing muffins. At the end of one path a woman looks at me, and does a double take. She waves me down, and I stop, my breath loud in my ears.

"Are you Abby Wambach? The soccer player?"

I'm in France! I think. *Are you serious?* My ego can't help but preen as I acknowledge that yes, I am. Silently I correct her—*I'm not a soccer player anymore*—but then I realize she's right. Soccer is no longer what I do, but it will always be a part of who I am, an indispensable thread of my past. I can't deny it any more than I can deny the labels I've claimed in this book: fraud, rebel, wife, advocate, failure, human—all of them. They'll always be there, stitched into my being, even as I make room for new labels, ones I've yet to discover and claim.

I wave to the woman and run off, anonymous once again. The maze unfurls itself before me, beckoning. I realize I know where I am, and how to find my way back.

ACKNOWLEDGMENTS

There are so many people in my life that inked the words to these pages. Your love and teachings and support are not lost on me. Thank you is wildly insufficient when it comes to my true, deep feelings for you all. I love you ALL.

My Family, My Body:

To Mom, Dad, Beth, Laura, Peter, Matt, Pat, Andy, Brooke, Tracy, all my in-laws and nieces and nephews . . . I have learned so many beautiful things along the way, and have felt your love and support through all my life adventures. Thank you for letting me go wander, yet always having a place to call HOME.

My chosen Family, My Spirit:

To Are, Dena, Kara, Syd, Sarah, Breaca, Audrey, Al . . . There are actually NO WORDS! You have carried my heart in yours, and the space you have allowed me to BE myself, and the learning and love I have felt in you have shaped the person I am, but more importantly the person I want to become. My love for you is unending.

My work Family, My Mind:

To Dan, all my teammates and coaches, Abbott, Julia, Sean . . . I have spent most of my adult life with you all, and I have learned a great many things. I've learned what hard work actually looks like, and that it sometimes isn't always pretty. I learned that no matter how badly you want to achieve anything in life, that the way in which you go about achieving it is actually the most important thing. Having this fierce integrity will always be with me for all of my life.

To THE love of my life . . .
Here is to the next 1000 years.

Many thanks also to the HarperCollins Children's Books team, including editor Alyson Day, publicist Lindsey Karl, marketing manager Meaghan Finnerty, production editor Emily Rader, designer Katie Fitch, and production manager Allison Brown.

ABOUT THE AUTHOR

ABBY WAMBACH is an American soccer player, a coach, a double Olympic gold medalist, a FIFA Women's World Cup champion, and the 2012 FIFA World Player of the Year. A six-time winner of the U.S. Soccer Athlete of the Year award, Wambach has been a regular on the U.S. women's national soccer team since 2003, earning her first cap in 2001. As a forward, she currently stands as the highest all-time goal scorer for the national team and holds the world record for international goals for both female and male soccer players, with 184 goals.